A FARCE TO BE RECKONED WITH

Roger Zelazny & Robert Sheckley

SPECTRA

BANTAM BOOKS
NEW YORK · TORONTO · LONDON · SYDNEY · AUCKLAND

c.1

Fiction
Zelazny, Roger

A FARCE TO BE RECKONED WITH
A Bantam Book / April 1995

SPECTRA *and the portrayal of a boxed "s" are trademarks of Bantam Books, a division of Bantam Doubleday Dell Publishing Group, Inc.*

Library of Congress Cataloging-in-Publication Data

Zelazny, Roger.
    A farce to be reckoned with / Roger Zelazny and Robert Sheckley.
      p.   cm.
    ISBN 0-553-37442-7
    I. Sheckley, Robert, 1928– . II. Title.
PS3576.E43F37   1995
813'.54—dc20   94-24508
                                                 CIP

Published simultaneously in the United States and Canada

Bantam Books are published by Bantam Books, a division of Bantam Doubleday Dell Publishing Group, Inc. Its trademark, consisting of the words "Bantam Books" and the portrayal of a rooster, is Registered in U.S. Patent and Trademark Office and in other countries. Marca Registrada. Bantam Books, 1540 Broadway, New York, New York 10036.

PRINTED IN THE UNITED STATES OF AMERICA
FFG   0 9 8 7 6 5 4 3 2 1

*To Nancy Applegate, in thanks for
blood, sweat, and tears*
                    Roger Zelazny

To my wife, Gail, with all my love
                    Robert Sheckley

PART ONE

Chapter 1

Ylith congratulated herself on her luck. She had chosen a perfect day for her journey from Heaven to the neat little graveyard outside of York, England. It was late May. The sunshine was glorious. Little birds of all sorts cavorted on mossy tree limbs, singing away on the edge of the surround. And the best of it was, the dozen little angels in her charge were being very good, even for angels.

The youngsters were playing together nicely, and Ylith was just starting to relax when suddenly a cloud of sulfurous yellow smoke puffed into existence not ten feet from her. When the smoke cleared, a short, red-haired fox-faced demon wrapped in a black cloak stood before her.

"Azzie!" Ylith cried. "What are you doing here?"

"I thought I'd take a little time off from infernal affairs, check out some shrines," Azzie said.

"Not thinking of changing your allegiance, are you?" Ylith asked.

"Not like you," Azzie said, referring to Ylith's former career as a witch. "Nice bunch you've got." He waved at the little angels.

"They're being terribly good, as you can see," Ylith remarked.

"It is not news when an angel acts good," Azzie said.

In fact, the little angels had begun running around the

graveyard and quarreling. Their voices rose, high-pitched and sugar sweet:

"Look what I've found! It's the tomb of St. Athelstan the Mealymouthed!"

"Oh, yeah? I've found the gravestone of St. Anne the Anxious, and she was much more important!"

The angels all looked very much alike with their snub features and their uniformly blond, smooth honey-colored hair that curled up beneath in the pageboy bob so fashionable that century. They all had plump wings, still covered with baby feathers and concealed under white and pink traveling cloaks. It was customary for angels visiting Earth to hide their wings.

Not that anyone would have been surprised to see angels in that year of 1324. It was well known that angels went back and forth between Earth and Heaven on a regular basis then, as did imps and devils and other supernatural creatures who had managed to remain in existence during the change of major deities, along with several anomalous immortal beings that no one had gotten around to identifying. In terms of deities, the Renaissance was an eclectic sort of an age.

"What are you doing here, Ylith?" Azzie asked.

The beautiful dark-haired witch explained that she had agreed to take this group of pubescent angels on a tour of Famous Shrines of England as part of their summer term Religious Training course. Ylith, perhaps because of her past history as a witch in the service of Bad—before she changed sides due to her love for a young angel named Babriel—was very much in favor of religious education for the young. They had to know something, so that when people asked questions, Heaven wouldn't be embarrassed by their answers.

Their starting point, the Martyr's Field in the north of

England, had many famous tombs; the little angels were busy discovering who had been planted where.

"Here's where they buried St. Cecily the Unwary," one of the little angels was saying. "I was talking to Cecily just the other day, in Heaven. She asked me to say a prayer at her grave."

Azzie said to Ylith, "The children seem to be doing fine. Why don't you come with me and let me give you some lunch?"

Ylith and Azzie had been an item once, back in the days when they were both Bad Creatures in service to Evil. Ylith still remembered how crazy she had been for the high-stepping, sharp-muzzled young fox demon. That was quite some time ago, of course.

Now she walked over to where Azzie indicated, near a spreading oak tree, and was more than a little surprised when a light flashed and the scene shifted abruptly. Suddenly she seemed to be standing on the shore of a great sea, with palm trees swaying on the beach and a big fat red sun lying low on the horizon. Near the edge of the water was a table laden with good things to eat and drink. And there was a broad bed, too, there on the beach, close to the table and made up with satin sheets and with innumerable cushions of all sizes and shapes and colors. Beside the bed a small chorus of satyrs sang the music of seduction.

"Just lie down over here," Azzie said, for he had accompanied Ylith into the new construct. "I will ply you with grapes and iced sherbets and we will know such delights as we once enjoyed—entirely too long ago."

"Hey, take it easy!" Ylith said, evading Azzie's amorous lunge. "You're forgetting I'm still an angel."

"No, I'm not," Azzie responded. "I just thought you might like to take a break."

"There are certain rules we must follow."

"How do they apply to your little fling with Dr. Faust?"

"That was a mistake," she said, "a case of bad judgment on my part while under emotional stress. Anyway, I repented afterwards. I'm okay. Just like before."

"Except that you and Babriel broke up over it."

"We still see each other. How did you hear about that, anyway?"

"The taverns of Limbo are the great exchange posts for Heavenly and Hellish news."

"I hardly see that my love life rates as particularly important gossip."

"Hey, you used to be big-time, lady. You used to hang out with me, remember?"

"Oh, Azzie, you're impossible," she said. "If you want to seduce me, you should be telling me how beautiful and desirable I am, not how important you are."

"As a matter of fact, you do look terribly good," Azzie said.

"And you are being terribly clever, as always," she said. She looked around at the seaside. "It is a beautiful illusion you've created here, Azzie. But I really must get back to the children."

She stepped out of the oceanside illusion, arriving back in the churchyard just in time to prevent Angel Ermita from pulling the ears of Angel Dimitri. Azzie soon appeared beside her, looking not too crestfallen for his recent rejection.

"Anyhow . . . I don't think it's me you want so much. What is bothering you, Azzie?" Ylith asked. "What are you doing here, really?"

"I'm between engagements," Azzie said with a bitter laugh. "I'm out of work. I came here to consider what to do next."

"Came here? To England?"

"To the Middle Ages, actually. It's one of my favorite periods of Earth history."

"How can you be out of work? I should think you'd be well employed by the Powers of Bad, especially after the masterful way you handled things in the recent Faust game."

"Ah! Don't talk to me about the Faust game!"

"Whyever not?"

"The judges of Hell have robbed me of the real honors I should have received after Mephistopheles bungled things so badly. The fools in Hell go on as though their positions are assured for all eternity, little realizing that they stand in imminent danger of going out of fashion and vanishing from men's thoughts forever."

"The Forces of Bad, on the verge of vanishing? But what would happen to Good?"

"It would vanish, too."

"That is quite impossible," Ylith said. "Mankind cannot live without firm opinions on Good and Bad."

"You think not? They did so once. The Greeks lived without absolutes, and so did the Romans."

"I'm not so sure of that," Ylith said. "But even if it's true, I can't imagine mankind living in that strident but morally bankrupt pagan way again."

"Why not?" Azzie asked. "Good and Bad aren't like bread and water. Mankind can get along nicely without them."

"Is that what you want, Azzie?" Ylith asked. "A world without Good or Bad?"

"Certainly not! Evil is my true work, Ylith, my vocation. I believe in it. What I want is to come up with something impressive in favor of what they call Bad, something that will motivate mankind, seize its attention, bring it back again to the dear old drama of Good and Bad, gain and loss."

"Do you think you can do that?" she asked.

"Of course. I don't want to boast, but I can do anything I set my mind to."

"At least," Ylith said, "you have no problem with your ego."

"If only I could get Ananke to see things my way!" Azzie said, referring to the personified spirit of Necessity who ruled gods and men in her inscrutable way. "But the silly old cow persists in her ambiguities."

"You'll think of something," Ylith said. "But now I really must be getting along."

"How can you stand being around those brats all the time?" Azzie asked.

"Getting yourself to like what you ought to like is half the trick of being good."

"And what is the other half?"

"Saying no to the blandishments of old boyfriends. Especially demonic ones! Good-bye, Azzie, and good luck."

Chapter 2

Disguised as a merchant, Azzie walked into the nearby city of York. Crowds were streaming toward a central point in the city, and he allowed himself to be carried along through the narrow winding streets. The people were in a holiday mood, but Azzie didn't know the cause of celebration.

A play was being enacted on a wooden platform in the middle of the city's central square; Azzie decided to watch. Stage plays for the general public were a fairly recent invention. Suddenly it had become a fad that was sweeping Europe.

It was all pretty simple and straightforward. Actors came out on a raised platform and pretended to be someone else. If you'd never seen it before it could be quite thrilling. Azzie had seen many plays in his time—a long time that stretched all the way back to the primitive goat dances of the ancient Hellenics—and he considered himself something of an expert. After all, he had been in the opening nights' audiences for Sophocles' great dramas. But this production in York was something different from goat dances and from Sophocles. This was realistic drama, and these two actors were talking like man and wife.

"So, Noah, what's new?" said Noah's wife.
"Woman, I have just had a divine revelation."

"Call that news?" Mrs. Noah said scornfully. "All you ever do, Noah, is walk out into the desert and have revelations. Isn't that true, children?"

"Sure is, Mama," said Jepthah.

"Right on," said Ham.

"Too true," said Shem.

"The Lord God has spoken to me," Noah said. "He commands me to take the boat I just built and move everyone aboard, because He is about to send a rain that will drown all things."

"How do you know this?" Mrs. Noah asked.

"I heard the voice of God."

"You and your crazy voices!" said Mrs. Noah. "If you think I'm going to move into that crazy boat with you and the kids just because you've heard a voice, you've got another think coming."

"I know it'll be a little crowded," Noah said, "especially after we get all the animals aboard. But not to worry. The Lord will provide."

"Animals?" Mrs. Noah asked. "You didn't say anything about animals."

"I was just getting to that part. That's what the Lord wants me to do. Save the animals from the Flood He's about to send."

"What animals are we talking about? Like pets?"

"God wants us to take more than just pets," Noah said.

"Like what?"

"Well, like everything," Noah said.

"How many of everything?"

"A pair of each kind of animal."

"Each kind? All of them?"

"That's the idea."

"You mean, like rats?"

"Yes, two of them."

"And rhinoceroses?"

"I admit it'll be a squeeze. But yes, rhinoceroses."

"And elephants?"

"We'll get them aboard somehow."

"And walruses?"

"Yes, of course, walruses too! God's instructions were very clear! Two of every kind."

Mrs. Noah gave Noah a look that as good as said, Poor drunken old Noah is having his fantasies again.

The audience loved it. There were about a hundred of them in the improvised theater, lounging on benches. They howled at Mrs. Noah's lines, stamping their feet to show approval. They were poor townspeople and rustics mostly, this audience that had gathered to watch a soon-to-be-apocryphal miracle play called *Noah*.

Azzie sat in one of the box seats that had been set up on a special scaffolding above and to the right of the stage. These seats were for the use of the prosperous citizen. From here he could watch the actors who played Noah's sons' wives changing their costumes. He could lounge at his ease and remain above the unwashed fetor of the masses for whom these plays, with their morally correct attitudes and their simpering points of argument, were intended.

The play went on. Noah boarded his boat; the rains began. A yokel with a watering can stood on a ladder and simulated the beginning of forty days and forty nights of rain. Azzie remarked to the well-dressed man in the box seat behind him, "Do what God says and everything will come out right for you! What a trivial conclusion, and how untrue to everyday life, where things come out in the oddest fashion with no regard for cause and effect."

"A sage point," the man said. "But consider, sir, these

tales are not meant to be true to life. They just point to how a man should attempt to comport himself in various circumstances."

"Well, obviously, sir," Azzie said. "But it is all sheerest propaganda. Don't you ever wish you could see a play with more invention in it, instead of a concoction like this that links homilies together as a butcher links sausages? Wouldn't you like to see a play whose plot was not hitched to the simpering determinism of standard morality?"

"Such would be refreshing, I suppose," the man said. "But such a philosophically based work is unlikely to come from the clerics who pen this sort of thing. Perhaps you'd care to pursue the point further, sir, after the play, over a tankard of ale?"

"Delighted," said Azzie. "I am Azzie Elbub, and my profession is gentleman."

"And I am Peter Westfall," the stranger said. "I am a grain importer, and I have my shop near St. Gregory's in the Field. But I see the players are beginning again."

The play got no better. After it was over, Azzie accompanied Westfall and several of his friends to the Sign of the Pied Cow, in Holbeck Lane near High Street. The landlord brought them flowing tankards, and Azzie ordered mutton and potatoes for all.

Westfall had received some education in a monastery in Burgundy. He was a large middle-aged man, sanguine of complexion, mostly bald, florid of gesture, and tending toward goutiness. From watching him refuse the meat, Azzie suspected him of vegetarianism, one of the deviant marks by which a Catharist heretic could be detected. It made no difference to Azzie, but he filed the information away for possible use some other time. Meanwhile there was the play to discuss with Westfall and the several other members of his party.

• • •

When Azzie complained about the play's lack of originality, Westfall said, "Indeed, sir, it is not supposed to be original. It is a story that tells a most edifying message."

"You call that an edifying message?" Azzie demanded. "Be patient and it'll all work out? You know perfectly well that the squeaky wheel gets the grease, and that if you don't complain nothing ever changes. In the Noah story, God was a tyrant. He should have been opposed! Who says God is right every time? Is a man to have no judgment of his own? If I were a playwright, I'd come up with something better than that!"

Westfall thought that Azzie's words were provocative and unorthodox, and it was in his mind to chastise him. But he noticed that there was a strange and commanding presence about the young fellow, and it was well known that members of the Court often disguised themselves as ordinary gentlemen, the better to draw responses from the unwary. So Westfall eased up on his queries, finally pleading the late hour as an excuse to retire.

After Westfall and the others had departed, Azzie stayed on awhile at the tavern. He wasn't sure what to do next. Azzie considered following Ylith and again trying his seductive wiles, but he realized it would not be a good move. He decided instead to travel on to the Continent, as he had originally intended. He was thinking of staging a play of his own. A play that would run counter to these morality plays with their insipid messages. An immorality play!

Chapter 3

The idea of staging an immorality play had seized and inflamed Azzie's imagination. He wanted to do great things, as he had in the past, first in the matter of Prince Charming and then again in the affair of Johann Faust. Now he wanted to strike again, to amaze the world, both spiritual and material.

A play! An immorality play! One that would create a new legend concerning man's destiny, and would single-handedly turn the tides of fortune toward Darkness!

He knew it was no small task; he knew he had some strenuous work ahead of him. But he also knew of the man who could help him create such a play: Pietro Aretino, one day to be eminent among Europe's Renaissance playwrights and poets. If Aretino could be convinced . . .

He made up his mind sometime after midnight. Yes, he would do it! Azzie walked through the town of York and out onto the fields. It was a splendid night, with a great spangling of stars shining from their fixed sphere. All good God-fearing folk had gone to bed hours ago. Seeing there was no one about, God-fearing or not, he stripped off his satin coat with the double row of buttons and opened his crimson waistcoat. He was splendidly muscled; supernatural creatures are able, by paying a modest fee, to keep their bodies in shape magically, utilizing the Hellish service that advertises "Sound body, evil mind." Stripped, he unfastened the linen binder that pulled his batlike demon's wings flat to his body in order to conceal them during his journeys among mankind. How good it felt to stretch his wings again! He used the linen binder to tie up his clothing to his back, taking care that his change was securely placed. He had lost money this way before through careless stowage. And then, with three running steps, he was aloft.

He slid forward in time as he went, enjoying its astringent smell. Soon he was over the English Channel, headed in a southeasterly direction. A brisk little following breeze pushed him along to the French coast in record time.

Morning found him above Switzerland, and he pumped for more altitude as the Alps came into sight. Next came the familiar Great St. Bernard Pass; soon after that he was flying over northern Italy. The air was noticeably warmer, even at Azzie's altitude.

Italy! Azzie loved it here. Italy was his favorite country, and the Renaissance, at which he had just arrived, his favorite time. He considered himself a sort of Renaissance demon. He flew over vineyards and tilled fields, little hills and sparkling rivers.

Azzie turned toward the east and, adjusting the set of his wings for the heavier air rising off the land, flew until land and sea seemed to interpenetrate in a great marsh that stretched green and gray below him and combined at last with the Adriatic. And here he came to the outskirts of Venice.

The final yellow rays of the setting sun illuminated the noble old city, glinting off the waters of the canals. In the oncoming gloom of evening he could just make out the gondolas, each with a lantern suspended from a pole in its rear, making their way back and forth over the Grand Canal.

Chapter 4

Back in York, old Meg the servant was cleaning up the inn when Peter Westfall arrived for his morning pail of ale.

"Master Peter," Meg said, "did you lose something last night? I found this where you gentlemen were sitting."

She handed him a little bag made of either deerskin or a very fine chamois. There was something inside.

"Oh, yes," Westfall said. He fumbled in his purse and found a farthing. "Here, have a pail of beer for your trouble."

Westfall returned to his house in Rotten Lane and went to his private room on the top floor. The room was spacious, with sloping windows set in the ceiling, and it was furnished with three tables made of stout oak. On these tables Westfall had placed various items of the alchemist's trade. In those days, the allied practices of alchemy and magic were accessible to many.

Westfall pulled out a chair and sat down. He untied the silver cord that knotted the throat of the bag, eased in two fingers, and carefully withdrew the smooth yellow stone he found inside. Engraved on it was a sign that could be recognized as the Hebrew letter, aleph.

Westfall knew it had to be a talisman or charm—an object of power. This was the sort of thing that a master magician would possess. With it, various conjuring powers would be his; he could call one or more spirits out of the deep, depending on how the talisman was tuned. Westfall had always wanted a talisman, for without it, his magic had always been quite ineffectual. He suspected that it had been dropped by the spooky young fellow he had talked with after the Noah play the previous night.

That gave him momentary pause. He stopped and thought. This, after all, was not his talisman. The owner would be likely to return for something so unusual and valuable. If he did, Westfall would of course return it immediately.

He started to put the talisman back into its soft case, then stopped. It could do no harm if he played with it until its owner returned. Surely that would be unobjectionable.

Westfall was all alone in his upper chamber. He turned to the talisman. "All right, let's get to work," he said. "I don't know which magical incantations to use, but if you're a genuine charmed object, a mere indication should be enough. Fetch me a spirit here to do my bidding and be quick about it."

Before his eyes the little stone talisman seemed to heave and sigh. The black sign on its side changed color, first becoming golden, then deepest red. It began to vibrate as if it had a small but powerful demon inside. A sort of high-pitched hum emanated from it.

The light in the chamber dimmed as if the talisman were stealing power from the sun. A whorl of dust rose from the floor and began to rotate in a counterclockwise direction. There were deep sounds apparently coming from the air, like unto the bellowing of impossibly large cattle. A cloud of green smoke filled the room, setting Westfall to coughing. While he caught his breath he watched the smoke dispel, revealing a young woman with lustrous black hair and an expression of pert beauty. She was wearing a long full skirt with many pleats, and a red silk blouse with dragons embroidered on it in thread of gold. She had on little high-heeled shoes, and a variety of tasteful jewelry. Right now she was very angry indeed.

"What is the meaning of this?" Ylith demanded. For it was Ylith whom the talisman had captured, probably because Azzie's last thoughts had been of her. The talisman must have picked up the impression.

"Why, I conjured you," Westfall said. "You are a spirit, and you must do my bidding. Right?" he added hopefully.

"Wrong," Ylith said. "I am an angel or a witch, not a mere spirit, and I am not bound to your talisman. I suggest that you recalibrate and try again."

"Oh, sorry," Westfall said, but as he spoke Ylith disappeared. Westfall said to the talisman, "Do be more careful this time. Fetch me the spirit you're supposed to. Do it!"

The talisman quivered as if it felt bad about being reprimanded. A musical note came from it, and then another. The light in the chamber dimmed again, then returned to full brilliance. There was a puff of smoke, and from it stepped a man wearing a complicated suit of dark satin and a conical hat. From his shoulders flowed a navy blue satin cloak embroidered all over with magical signs in gold thread. The man had a mustache and beard, and he looked entirely out of sorts.

"What is it?" he asked. "I told everyone I was not to be disturbed until after my next sequence of experiments. How can I be expected to pursue my investigations unless I am left in peace? Who are you and what do you want?"

"I am Peter Westfall," Westfall said. "I have conjured you by the power of this talisman." Westfall held it up.

The bearded gentleman said, "You conjured me? What

are you talking about? Let me see that!" He looked closely
at the talisman. "Originally Egyptian, but familiar somehow. Unless I miss my guess this is one of the original series with which King Solomon bound a larger collection of
spirits back quite some time ago. I thought all of these had
been retired. Where did you get this?"

"Never mind," Westfall said. "I have it. That's the important thing, and you must obey me."

"I must, must I? We'll just see about that!" The man
suddenly doubled in size and moved threateningly toward
Westfall. Westfall seized the talisman and squeezed it; Hermes let out a shriek and stepped back.

"Take it easy!" he said. "You don't have to get rough."

"This charm gives me power over you!"

"Oh, I suppose it does," the other responded. "But
damn it, this is ridiculous! I'm a former Greek god and a
supreme magician — Hermes Trismegistus, by name."

"Well, you've come a cropper this time, Hermes,"
Westfall said.

"That seems to be the case," Hermes said. "Who are
you? Not a magician, that I'm sure of." He looked around.
"And no king, because this is certainly no palace. You're
some sort of commoner, aren't you?"

"I am a grain merchant," Westfall said.

"And how did you come by this amulet?"

"None of your business."

"Probably found it in your granny's attic!"

"It doesn't matter where I got it!" Westfall's fist tightened convulsively over the amulet.

"Take it easy!" Hermes said, wincing. "All right, that's
better." Hermes took a deep breath and performed a small
incantation to calm himself down. This was no time for
rage, no matter how justified. This stupid mortal did indeed
have power over him because of this ancient amulet. How

had he gotten it? The fellow must have stolen it, because he obviously knew little or nothing about the Art.

"Master Westfall," Hermes said, "I acknowledge your power over me. I do indeed have to obey you. Tell me what it is you want, and let us waste no further time."

"That's more like it," Westfall said. "First I want a sack of gold coins, fine minted and capable of being spent where and how I please. English, Spanish, or French coins will do nicely, but no Italian ones—they always clip the edges. I also want an Old English sheepdog, a pedigreed one like the King has. That'll do for a start, but I'll have more requests after that."

"Not so fast," Hermes said. "How many wishes are you expecting me to grant?"

"As many as I want!" Westfall cried. "Because I've got the amulet!" He flourished it, and Hermes winced with pain.

"Not so hard! I'll get your stuff! Give me a day or two!" And so saying, Hermes disappeared.

Hermes had no difficulty putting together the items Westfall wanted. He kept bags and bags of gold coin in a cave under the Rhine, in the care of dwarfs who had been out of work since Götterdämmerung. The Old English sheepdog was no great trouble, either—Hermes easily kidnapped one from a kennel near Spottiswode. Then he returned to Westfall's chamber in York.

Chapter 5

"**G**ood dog. Now go lie in the corner," Westfall said. The half-grown Old English sheepdog looked at him and barked.

"He's not very well trained," Westfall said.

"Hey, you didn't say anything about him being trained," Hermes replied. "He's got a pedigree as long as your arm."

"He's a good-looking dog," Westfall acknowledged, "and the gold pieces are satisfactory." He had a mess of them in a small stout leather bag at his feet.

"I'm glad you're satisfied," Hermes said. "Now if you will just tell this amulet that you release me and that I am no longer in your power, we can each of us get on with our own business."

"Not so fast!" Westfall said. "I still have a number of wishes I want you to grant."

"But I'm busy!" Hermes complained.

"You must be patient. I'll need you around for a while longer, my dear Trismegistus, and if you do what I ask, after that I'll consider releasing you."

"That's not fair!" Hermes said. "I'm willing to grant you a wish or two out of respect for your ill-gotten talisman, but you're taking advantage of the situation."

"Magic is there to take advantage of people with," Westfall said.

"Don't press your luck," Hermes said. "You don't know what you're playing around with here."

"Enough of this talk," Westfall said. "Listen carefully, Hermes. Earlier, before I conjured you, the talisman gave me somebody else. A woman. A very beautiful woman. Do you know who I'm talking about?"

Hermes Trismegistus closed his eyes and concentrated. Then he opened his eyes again.

"My sense of postcognition tells me you conjured up one of God's angels, a former witch named Ylith."

"How did you know that?" Westfall asked.

"Second sight is one of my attributes," Hermes said. "If you'll release me, I'll teach you the way of it."

"Never mind. What I want is for you to bring that lady —Ylith, you called her? I want you to bring her to me."

"I doubt she'll want to come," Hermes said, eyeing Westfall with interest. This was a twist he hadn't anticipated.

"I don't care if she wants to or not," Westfall said. "The sight of her has inflamed my imagination. I want her."

"Ylith is going to love this," Hermes remarked aside. He knew she was a strong-minded lady who had been fighting for feminine spiritual equality in the cosmos long before the concept was even conceived of on Earth.

"She will have to get used to me," Westfall said. "I intend to possess that lady in all the ways a man may possess a maid."

"I can't make her agree to that," Hermes said. "There's a limit to my powers; they stop at having any influence over the feminine psyche."

"You don't have to make her agree to anything," Westfall said. "I'll do that myself. You merely have to put her in my power."

Hermes thought for a while, then said, "Westfall, I

have to be frank with you. Possession of magic has over-
borne your good sense. This thing with Ylith is not a good
idea. You're meddling with something here you don't want
to get anywhere near."

"Be silent! Do as I say!" His eyes were wide and shining.

"Have it your own way," Hermes said, and he conjured himself out of there, marveling at the unerring way
humans had of getting themselves into trouble. And he was
beginning to see the glimmering of a plan that might bring
benefit to himself and the other Olympians who were now
cooped up in the unreal world known as Afterglow. But
first he was going to have to procure Ylith for Westfall, and
that might prove more than a little difficult.

Chapter
6

Hermes took himself to one of his favorite places, an old shrine on the Aegean island of Delos that had been dedicated to his worship for some thousands of years. Here he sat down and, looking over the wine-dark sea, considered his situation.

Although he was one of the original twelve Olympians, Hermes hadn't suffered the fate of the other gods when the entire Greek thing collapsed shortly after the death of Alexander the Great and the birth of superstitious rationalism in Byzantium. The other gods hadn't been able to fit into the new world that came into being with Hellenistic times, and when the new religion came along, they hadn't stood a chance. Their worshipers all abandoned them; they were declared not to exist, and were forced to lead a shadowy existence in the realm called Afterglow. Afterglow was a dreary place, almost exactly like the ancient Greek underworld. Hermes was glad he didn't have to live there.

Hermes was held over from the ancient Greek world because of his long association with magic. From early times he had been active in the conjuring arts, and a body of lore had sprung up that was attributed to his inspiration. The Corpus Hermeticum, ascribed to Cornelius Agrippa and others, had become the soul of Renaissance magic; Hermes was its presiding deity.

He had proven useful to mankind in other ways, too.

He was fine at locating things, and he had been long associated with medicine due to the caduceus he often carried, a souvenir of his Egyptian days as Thoth.

He was basically a friendly god, more approachable than most. Over the years he had entered into discussions with many human magicians, all of whom had conjured him with respect. But this was the first time anyone had ever conjured him by force, causing him to obey whether he wanted to or not. He didn't like it. Trouble was, he didn't know quite what to do about it.

He was brooding over this, sitting under a great oak tree and looking out to sea, when he heard a soft, whispering sound. He listened more carefully. A voice was saying to him, "My boy, what seems to be the trouble?"

Hermes said, "Zeus, is that you?"

"Yes, it's me," Zeus said, "but only as a ghostly essence. The real me is in Afterglow, where all the rest of us were banished. All except you, of course."

"It wasn't my fault they carried me over as Hermes Trismegistus," Hermes said.

"No one is blaming you, my son. Just stating a fact."

"I don't understand how you can be here at all," Hermes said. "Even as a ghostly essence."

"I have a special dispensation. I can manifest my essence wherever oak trees flourish, and that's not bad, given the circumstances I'm in nowadays and the prevalence of oaks. Something seems to be troubling you. What is it, Hermes? You can tell your old dad."

Hermes hesitated. He didn't trust Zeus. None of the Olympians did. They remembered what he had done to Cronus, his father—castrated the poor old bugger and thrown his parts into the sea. They knew that Zeus feared the same fate, and so they tended to make sure no one was in a position to do that to him. Even the thought of it made him touchy, and if he was treacherous and inconstant, it was because he thought that was the safest way to keep his *cojones*. Hermes knew all this, but he also knew that Zeus was a good person to talk to. "Father Zeus, a human has gotten control of me."

"Indeed? How could that have happened?"

"Remember those seals that King Solomon bound some of the fellows with? Well, they haven't all been retired."

Hermes told him the story, adding at the end, "So what can I do?"

Zeus rustled his leaves and said, "This human pretty well has you right now. Play along, but watch what goes on. When something happens that you can use, then you must act immediately and drastically."

"I know all this," Hermes said. "Why are you stating the obvious?"

"Because I know your scruples, my son. You've gone along with these new people and their complicated ideas about the old gods. You've been taken in by their big talk. You think it's all very profound, this magic stuff of theirs. Well, let me just tell you, it's all a matter of power, that's all magic is, and power is nine tenths a matter of trickery."

"All right, enough already," Hermes said. "How am I supposed to get hold of this witch woman for Westfall?"

"That is the easiest of the problems that face you. Go to your sister Aphrodite and ask her for the use of Pandora's box. She's been using it for her jewelry lately. It will make a first-rate spirit catcher."

"Of course, a spirit catcher! What will I do with it?"

"You're the great magician. Figure it out for yourself."

Some time later, Hermes appeared in the graveyard in York, disguised as an eccentric old gentleman. Under his arm was a parcel, neatly wrapped in brown paper and tied with twine. He walked up to Ylith and said in an altered voice, "Miss Ylith? Your friend asked that I give you this."

"Azzie left a present for me?" Ylith said. "How nice!"

She stripped away the wrapping and opened the box without thinking. In the lid was a mirror, a sparkly, hazy, multicolored mirror of a type she remembered seeing in Babylonia and in Egypt, a magic mirror, a soul catcher, damn it, someone had pulled that old trick on her! Quickly she averted her eyes, but it was too late; her soul, flying out of her mouth at that instant like a tiny transparent butterfly, was caught by the mirror and pulled in, and in that moment Ylith's body collapsed. Hermes caught her and lowered her gently to the ground. Then he closed the cover of the box with a decisive snap. When he had Pandora's box safely secured with a woven golden cord, he gave a pair of lunching workmen a coin to pick up the body and transport it across town to Westfall's chambers. "Careful, there! Don't damage it!" The workmen seemed a bit puzzled and not at all sure they were doing the right thing until Hermes told them he was a doctor who could revive the unfortunate lady, who obviously had suffered a shock brought about by baleful zodiacal influences. Hearing so plausible and scientific an explanation, none of the workmen inquired any further. After all, they were just following doctor's orders.

Chapter
7

Westfall wondered what was taking Hermes so long, but he decided it might not be so easy a matter to take a woman away from the world, just like that. He wondered at himself; it wasn't his usual way of doing things. Had some supernatural creature established an influence over him and indicated to him by subtle means that he should ask for the woman? He wasn't sure, but he sensed the operation here of something abnormal, something beyond the laws of magic, something that worked in its own way and revealed itself or not as it saw fit.

The long afternoon passed; Westfall found a bit of cheese in his pantry, and a heel of bread. He moistened the bread with some of last night's soup, heated over a little stove he kept in a corner. A draft of wine washed it down, and then he dozed in his armchair. It was a peaceful time until a sound as of the air splitting apart came to his ears. He sprang to his feet, crying, "Have you brought the woman?"

"I have done my part," Hermes said. He waved his hand to dispel the clouds of smoke that had attended his arrival. He was dressed as before, but this time he carried under his arm a small, richly made wooden box.

"What have you got there?" Westfall asked.

Just then came the sound of heavy footsteps on the stairs. A muffled voice from outside cried, "Will somebody please get the door?" Westfall went and opened it. Two large workmen came in, lugging between them the body of a beautiful young woman, unconscious, and pale as death.

"Where do you want her?" asked the workman carrying the end with the head and shoulders.

"Just put her down on the couch over there. Gently!"

Hermes paid both workmen and saw them to the door. He said to Westfall, "I have given her into your power. Now you have her body. But I advise you not to fool around with it without the lady's permission."

"Where is she?" Westfall asked. "Her consciousness, I mean?"

"You mean her soul," Hermes said. "It is right here in this box." He put the box down on one of Westfall's tables. "Open it when you please, and her soul will fly out and reanimate her body. But watch your step. The lady is more than a little angry, not taking kindly to being conjured when she was trying to do something else."

"Her soul is really in the box?" Westfall asked. He lifted the small brown silver-inlaid container and shook it. From deep within he heard a shriek and a muffled curse.

"You're on your own now," Hermes said.

"But what am I supposed to do?"

"That's for you to find out."

Westfall picked up the box and shook it gently. He said, "Miss Ylith? Are you in there?"

"You bet I'm here, you unspeakable piglike thing," Ylith said. "Open this lid so I can get out and get at you."

Westfall turned pale and squeezed the lid down tightly with both hands. "Oh, dear." He looked at Hermes.

Hermes shrugged.

"She's angry."

"You're telling me?" Hermes said.

"But what am I to do with her?"

"You wanted her," Hermes pointed out. "I thought you'd have that part figured out."

"Well, not exactly."

"I'd advise you to try to come to some understanding with her. You're going to have to do that."

"Maybe I'll just put the box away for a while," said Westfall.

"That would be a mistake."

"Why?"

"Unless Pandora's box is watched all of the time, what is within is able to get out."

"That's not fair!"

"I've played fair with you, Westfall. You should know these things always have a trick to them. Good luck."

He began to make a gesture to conjure himself out of there.

"Remember," Westfall said, "I still have the talisman. I can call you up when I wish!"

"I wouldn't advise trying it," Hermes said, and vanished.

Westfall waited until Hermes' smoke had faded away. Then he turned to the box. "Miss Ylith?"

"What is it?"

"Could we have a talk, you and I?"

"Open this box and let me out. I'll give you talk."

Westfall shuddered at the sound of rage in her voice. "Maybe we should wait a little while," he said. "I need to think this out." Ignoring her curses, he walked to the other end of the chamber and settled down to think. But he didn't take his eyes off the box.

Westfall kept the box on his nightstand. He did have to sleep occasionally, but he wakened himself periodically to make sure Ylith was still in there; he had become concerned that she would get out on her own. He began to dream that she was about to open the box, or that it had opened during the night. Sometimes he woke up screaming.

"Listen, miss," he said, "what say we forget all about this? I'll let you go and you leave me alone. Is that okay?"

"No," Ylith said.

"Why? What do you want?"

"Indemnity," Ylith said. "You can't expect things to happen as easily as that, Westfall."

"What will you do if I let you out?"

"I don't honestly know."

"You won't kill me, though, will you?"

"I might. I just might."

It was a standoff.

Chapter 8

Pietro Aretino was somewhat surprised to find a red-haired demon at his door that day in Venice in 1524. But not too surprised. Aretino made it a point never to be put out of countenance by anything.

He was a big man, his own red hair receding from his high brow. Thirty-two years old that month, he had spent all his adult life as a poet and playwright. His verses, which combined the utmost scurrility with an exquisite sense of rhyme, were recited and sung from one corner of Europe to the other.

Aretino was able to live well on the expensive presents that kings, noblemen, and prelates were forever forcing upon him to induce him to desist from attacking and mocking them. "Pray take this gold salver, good Aretino, and be so kind as to disinclude me in your latest broadside."

Aretino had been expecting something of the sort when the knocking came on his door. He opened it himself, his servant having gone home for the day. One look told him that this fellow who stood before him was no Earthly messenger. No, this foxy-faced and bright-eyed personage had that air about him of one of the supernatural ones that Aretino had always heard about but had not up until now met.

"Good evening to you, sir," Aretino said, keeping a

respectful tone until he knew whom he was insulting. "Have you some business with me? For I think I have not seen your face."

"We have not met before this," Azzie said. "Yet it seems to me that I know the Divine Aretino through the luscious sagacity of his verses, in which a sound moral point is never far behind the laughter."

"It is good of you to say so, sir," said Aretino. "But many hold that there is no moral content whatsoever to my lines."

"They are deceived," Azzie said. "To scoff at the pretensions of mankind, as you unerringly do, dear master, is to point up the excellencies of that which the churchmen are usually all too willing to dismiss."

"You speak out boldly, sir, in favor of those deeds that men consider evil."

"Yet men perform the Seven Deadly Sins with an alacrity they do not display in their high-minded quests for the good. Even Sloth is entered into with a greater alacrity than accompanies the pursuits of piety."

"Sir," said Aretino, "your viewpoint is my viewpoint. But let us not remain here on the doorstep, gossiping like a pair of old crones. Come into my house, and let me pour you a glass of a fine wine I recently brought back from Tuscany."

Aretino led Azzie inside. His house, or rather his palazzo, was small though luxurious. The floors were carpeted with thick-piled rugs sent by the Doge himself; tall waxen tapers burned in bronze candelabra, and the flames sent streaks of light down the cream-colored walls.

Aretino led the way to a low-ceilinged sitting room decorated with rugs and wall hangings. A charcoal brazier took off the wintry chill that still hung in the air. He gestured to Azzie to make himself comfortable and poured him a glass of sparkling red wine from the crystal decanter that stood on a little inlaid table nearby.

"Now then, sir," said Aretino, after they had toasted each other's health, "tell me how I may be of service to you."

"Say rather," said Azzie, "that I wish to be of service to you, since you are the preeminent poet and satirist in Europe and I am but a simple patron of the arts who wishes to set forth an artistic enterprise."

".What exactly did you have in mind, sir?" Aretino asked.

"I would like to produce a play."

"What an excellent idea!" cried Aretino. "I have several that might suit your purposes very nicely. Allow me to fetch the manuscripts."

Azzie held up a hand. "Although I have no doubt as to the supreme perfection of everything you have written, my dear Aretino, something already written will not do. I would like to be involved in a new enterprise, a piece that would make use of a particular conception of mine."

"Of course," Aretino said, for he was familiar with men who wished to produce works of art, coming up themselves with the conception but leaving the dull work of the actual writing to someone else. "And what, sir, do you propose for the theme?"

"I would like my play to point up some simple home truths," Azzie said. "These are facts of existence that experienced men have known throughout the centuries, yet they are not so acknowledged by our dramatists. These writers I refer to, slavishly following Aristotle, insist upon proving the banalities: that the wages of sin are death, that gluttons end up in the gutter, that the lascivious are doomed to disappointment, and that those who love lightly are condemned never to love well."

"These are the usual sorts of moral propositions," Aretino said. "Do you wish to confute them?"

"Indeed I do," Azzie said. "Even though they are the very stuff of everyday folk wisdom, some of us know that matters do not always come out this way. My play would prove the contrary to what is generally maintained by the mumble-mouthed do-gooders. In my play, the Seven Deadly Sins will be shown as the true path to a fine life, or in any event, as no impediment to it. In brief, my dear Aretino, I wish to produce an immorality play."

"What a noble conception!" cried Aretino. "Oh, I applaud you, sir, for your great notion that single-handedly attempts to oppose the centuries of mealymouthed propaganda with which men have tried to convince themselves to do the conventional thing no matter how they opposed it. But let me point out, sir, that it will be difficult to mount such a production without bringing down upon our heads the hypocritical wrath of Church and State. And besides, where will we find a cast? Or a stage that isn't claimed by the Church?"

"In the play I want to produce," said Azzie, "I do not contemplate such a formal procedure as actors, stage, and audience. The play will unfold naturally; we will give our actors a general sense of the situation, and let them work out the lines and action for themselves, in a free-form and unpremeditated manner."

"But how would you have your play prove its moral unless you foreplan the outcome?"

"I have a few thoughts on that," Azzie said, "which I will share with you when we are in agreement on the project. Let me just say that the machinery of worldly cause and effect is something I can manipulate to good advantage to get the results I desire."

"It would take a supernatural being to make such a statement," said Aretino.

"Listen to me closely," Azzie said.

"I listen," said Aretino, somewhat taken aback by Azzie's suddenly commanding manner.

"I am Azzie Elbub, a demon of noble lineage, at your service, Aretino," Azzie said, making a negligent gesture with one hand, at the end of which blue sparks of lightning flashed.

Aretino's eyes opened wide. "Black magic!"

"I avail myself of these infernal stage effects," said Azzie, "so that you might know at once with whom you are dealing."

Drawing his fingers together, Azzie produced a large emerald, then another, and another. He turned out six of them and lay them side to side on the little table where the wine stood. Then he made a pass over them, and the emeralds shuddered and collapsed into a single large stone, the largest emerald the world had ever known.

"Amazing!" said Aretino.

"It must return to its original form after a while," Azzie said. "But the effect is pretty, is it not?"

"Amazing!" said Aretino again. "Can such a trick be taught?"

"Only to another demon," said Azzie. "But there is a lot I can do for you, Aretino. Come into this enterprise with me and not only will you be paid beyond your wildest dreams, but also you will receive a tenfold increase in your already sizable fame because you will be the author of a play that will set forth a new legend upon this old Earth. With a little luck, it will presage the beginning of an age of candor such as the hypocritical old globe has not yet seen."

Azzie's eyes flashed fire as he spoke—he wasn't one to stint his effects when trying to make a point.

Aretino stumbled back at this display. He tripped over a footstool and would have fallen heavily had not Azzie reached out a long lean arm covered in fine red hair and restored the surprised poet to his balance.

"I can't tell you how flattered I am," Aretino said, "that you would come to me for this supreme production. I am entirely in accord with your wishes, my dear Lord Azzie, but the matter isn't quite so simple. I would not give you less than the best. Give me a week's time, my lord, in which I may consider the matter, and meditate, and consult the ancient stories and legends I have heard. The entire basis for this play of yours, however it is mounted, must be a story. It is the search for that story to which I'll devote myself. Shall we say until next week at this same time?"

"That is most excellently said," Azzie said. "I am glad you are not jumping into this matter lightly. Yes, take a week."

With that, Azzie made a gesture and vanished.

PART TWO

Chapter 1

When a demon leaves Earth in order to go to the Realm of Darkness, profound forces are involved, discernible only to senses that can detect what for most humans is undetectable. That evening, not long after his talk with Aretino, Azzie gazed upward at the starry sky. He snapped his fingers—he had recently procured a new finger-snapping spell, and now was a good chance to try it out. The spell kicked in and flung him into the air, and soon he was traveling rapidly through space, his passage brighter than a falling star.

Azzie roared through the transparent separation that forms the covering of the Heavenly sphere of the heavens, picking up mass as he went in accordance with the law of speeding objects that governs even devils in their flight. The stars seemed to nod and wink at his passage. The wind that howled between the worlds sent a chill through him, and Ur-frost formed on his nose and eyebrows. He felt the savage chill of those desolate spaces, but he didn't slow down. He was in the devil's own hurry. Once Azzie got an idea, he was unstoppable.

In order to get a great event like an immorality play written and staged, he needed money. He had to pay the human actors, and it cost plenty to purchase the special effects—those fortuitous miracles that would occur to cheer his actors on their way to undeserved good fortune. Azzie had remembered that he hadn't been paid his bonus for the Bad Deed of the Year award which he had received for his part in the Faust affair.

At last his speed was sufficient for the great shift that propels a being from one realm of existence into another. Suddenly Azzie was no longer traveling through the sphere of mundane objects and energies made up of atoms and their constituent member particles. He had passed through the invisible and impalpable separation that divides ordinary objects like mu-mesons and tachyons from the finer particles of the Spiritual Realm.

He found himself in a place of great misty shapes and indistinct colors, where vast and indistinct objects swam in a honey-colored atmosphere. He was home again.

Just ahead of him were the great grim blue-black walls of Hell City, on which the walls of ancient Babylon had been modeled. Sentinel devils patrolled the high bastions; Azzie waved his pass at them and hurtled on.

He came in over the dark Satanic suburbs and soon was in the business section of Hell City, where the administrative work was carried out. He passed by the Public Works division; it was of no interest to him just now. The great bureaucratic buildings coalesced around him, he picked the right one, and soon he was hurrying down a corridor filled with other demons, as well as imps in pageboy's uniforms. Here and there were the inevitable kimono-clad succubi who made the lunches of senior officials so pleasant. He came at last to the Accounting Section.

He was expected to take his place at the end of the long line of petitioners who waited impatiently for someone to hear their cases. They were a down-at-the-heels and seedy bunch. Azzie went right past them to the head of the line, flourishing a gold-edged Bypass Card he had gotten from Asmodeus back when he stood high in that senior devil's favor.

The clerk in charge of Payments Past Due was an ill-favored Transylvanian imp-goblin with a long nose and breath that was horrific even by Hell's standards. Devoted as he and all his fellows were to doing as little as possible, thus saving their own energy and Hell's money, he claimed that Azzie had not filled in his papers correctly, and in any event, he had filled out the wrong forms. Azzie showed him a Waiver of Correctness signed by Beelzebub himself. It stated that no impediment in the paperwork was to stop or delay the payment of moneys owed to said demon. The imp-goblin was sore pressed by this, but found a last excuse.

"I do not have the authority to pass on these things. I'm just a wretched little imp-goblin clerk. What you've got to do is go down the hall, take the first door to your right, go up the staircase—"

Azzie was having none of it. He produced another form, an Instant Action Chit, which stated that no excuses would be tolerated in the paying of this demand, and that any obfuscation on the part of the requisite clerk would be met with Pecuniary Punishment, viz., taking the amount owed out of the clerk's own salary. This was the most drastic form of action anyone could take in Hell City, and Azzie had had to steal the form from the special office where they were handed out only to the favored few.

The form's effect on the imp-goblin was immediate and gratifying. "It's not coming out of my pocket!" the imp-goblin said. "Where's my stamp?" He rummaged around his desk, found it, and stamped Azzie's papers with URGENT! PAY IMMEDIATELY! in letters of fire. "Now just take that down the hall to the Payments window. And then kindly go away. You have quite ruined my day."

Azzie did so. He vowed to return with nasty new tricks if there was any further trouble. But the clerk at the Payments window, seeing the notation PAY IMMEDIATELY!, initialed it and handed over forthwith and without delay several sacks of gold coins, making up the full amount of what Azzie was owed.

Chapter
2

By the time Azzie got back to Venice, six days of Earth-time had passed. The weather had turned mild and glorious, and flowering plants had burst into bloom in the little parks. White and yellow blooms were everywhere, glorious in the mild sunshine. The ladies of Venice promenaded in the fine weather, the men walking along with them, prattling of the affairs of nobles and their ladies. The tide was falling, carrying the garbage and debris of the inhabitants out to sea. The spanking east wind was sweeping out the odorous vapors that made Venice a likely place for European plagues to begin. All in all it was a good time to be alive.

Azzie had planned to look into the Arsenal, the most famous shipbuilding facility in Europe, but no sooner had he turned into a narrow cobblestoned street that led to it than he bumped into a large blue-eyed fellow who took one look at him and gave him a warm thump on the back.

"Azzie! Upon my word, it is you, isn't it?" said the other.

It was the angel Babriel, an old acquaintance from by-gone adventures. Although they served opposite sides in the great battle of Light and Dark, they had become friends — or if not exactly friends, something closer than acquaintances — over the course of events. They had another connection, too—the love they both bore the beautiful black-haired witch named Ylith.

Azzie thought that Babriel, who worked nowadays for Michael the Archangel, might be here in Venice to keep an eye on him, and might even be suspecting him—through some previously unheard-of Heavenly art—of the scheme he was attempting to hatch.

After Babriel expressed surprise at Azzie's presence in Venice, Azzie replied, "I took a little time off from my duties in Hell to enjoy the sights of this fair city. It is surely the Earthly paradise of the present generation."

"It was wonderful to see you again," Babriel said to Azzie, "but now I must rejoin the others. The angel Israfel comes at vespers to pick us up and return us to Heaven, this being only a weekend outing."

"Good journey to you, then," Azzie said.

And so they parted. Azzie had picked up no intimation that Babriel was spying on him, yet he wondered why the blue-eyed angel was in Venice at just this time.

Chapter 3

Babriel always enjoyed getting back to Heaven. It was such a pretty place, with its rows of small white houses on generous green lawns, its fine old trees, and its general air of genteel Goodness. Not all of Heaven looked like that, of course, but this was West Heaven, the better side of Paradise, where the archangels lived and where the Spiritual Embodiments had summer places. The Spiritual Embodiments were tall and attractive women, and an angel could do far worse for himself than tie up with one of them —for the mating of excellent qualities was allowed in Heaven. But as beautiful as they were, Babriel wasn't attracted to them in the way of a man and a maid. His heart went out to Ylith. Perhaps because of her previous history as Whore of Athens and Assistant Whore of Babylon, back when she served Bad, he found her irresistible. Ylith sometimes seemed in love with Babriel, sometimes not.

He went by a shortcut to East Heaven and stopped at Ylith's house, just to say hello, but she was not in. A refurbished nature spirit gotten up like a cherub was mowing the lawn, a penance he had imposed on himself for past indiscretions. He told Babriel that Ylith was away leading a group of young angels to sacred shrines on Earth.

"Oh, really?" Babriel said. "What period are they visiting?"

"I believe it's called the Renaissance," said the nature spirit.

Babriel thanked him and left in a thoughtful mood. Was it merely coincidence that Azzie was also visiting that period? Babriel was not suspicious by nature, and was considered trusting even for an angel. But he had learned the hard way that, strange though it might seem, everybody was not like him. Especially not Azzie, in whom dissimulation was such a second nature as to overshadow entirely his first nature, whatever that might be. Babriel had his doubts as to Ylith's orthodoxy, despite her enthusiasm for every sort of Niceness. He didn't think she would turn away from her allegiance to Heaven, but she might have been tempted to look up her old boyfriend—or, more likely, he her. If that was the case, why had they picked the Renaissance in which to rendezvous? Or was it just coincidence?

Babriel was brooding on these matters when he walked up Shady Olive Tree Lane and came to the big white mansion on top of the hill where Michael lived. The archangel was tending to the roses in his front yard, the sleeves of his white linen gown pushed back to reveal his brawny forearms.

"Welcome back, Babriel!" said the archangel, putting down his clippers and wiping from his brow the sweet sweat of honest labor. "Did you enjoy your sojourn in Venice?"

"Immeasurably, sir. I took the opportunity of trying to improve my knowledge of the arts. For the greater glory of Good, of course."

"Of course," said Michael, with a friendly twinkle to his deep-set eyes.

"I ran into Azzie Elbub, sir."

"Saw old Azzie, did you?" said Michael, stroking his chin thoughtfully. He remembered the demon well from their last encounter during the affair of Johann Faust. "What was he up to?"

"He said he was just there for a little holiday from his duties in Hell, though I suspect he might have come there to be near the angel Ylith. She is also on Earth."

"It's possible," said Michael. "Or there could be some other reason."

"Like what, sir?"

"There are many possibilities," Michael said vaguely. "I shall have to think about this. Meanwhile, if you're quite rested, there's a lot of correspondence to take care of inside." Michael was punctilious about answering his fan mail, which came to him from all over the Spiritual Realm, and from Earth as well.

"I'll get right to it," Babriel said. He hurried inside to his little office in what had been the Servants' Wing but was now called the Honored Guests of Lesser Importance Wing.

PART THREE

Chapter
1

I t was a special embarrassment for Ylith to find herself shut up in a box. She hadn't had that one tried on her since the infatuated King Priam of Troy had constructed a special box in which he hoped to put Ylith once he caught her. But he never caught her. And now Troy was long gone, and Priam along with it, and Ylith was still here, at least partially because she didn't put her head into boxes.

It only goes to show you, she thought, no sense being too proud. Just look at me now. In a box.

A pale luminous glow filled the box, revealing fields, hedges, and a line of mountains in the background.

She heard a man's soft voice at her ear.

"Ylith, what are you doing here? You seem to be in trouble. Let me help."

The lights in the box came up brighter.

"Who am I talking to?" Ylith asked.

"It's Zeus," the voice said. "I can still do things like that, even in my present reduced circumstances. But you haven't told me what you're doing here."

"Some guy kidnapped me and locked me up in here." Ylith had met Father Zeus once before, when she had been trying out for a part as a nature spirit during the Greek Revival period in Rome. Zeus had said he'd let her know, and she hadn't thought about it since.

"Why won't he let you out?" Zeus asked.

"He's afraid I'll kill him. And I will, too!"

Zeus sighed. "You sound like my daughter, Artemis. Talk about implacable! Why not try a little dissimulation?"

"What do you mean?"

"Tell this kidnapper you like the idea of being locked up in a box by him."

"He'd never believe that!"

"Try it. Kidnappers are goofy. Tell him anything. Just get free."

"You mean lie?"

"Of course."

"That wouldn't be honest!"

"You could make amends later. That's what I always did, when I remembered. Meanwhile, you'd be free."

"But we're not supposed to lie," Ylith said, though her voice was irresolute.

"Now, my dear, talk again to this human and get him to see things your way. Get back out into the world. You're too pretty to stay shut up in a box."

Later, after she had composed herself and looked to her makeup, Ylith cried out, "Westfall? You still there?"

"Yes, I'm here."

"Aren't you supposed to be at work or something?"

"Of course. But frankly, I'm afraid of leaving you alone. I mean, maybe you could get out—or at least enchant me."

"I could enchant you anyhow," Ylith said in a sultry voice. "But you really think I'm such a vicious witch?"

"Well," Westfall said, "after you lit into me as you did, I figured I'd better be prepared for the worst."

"You got me sore," Ylith said. "No woman likes to be suddenly snatched out of what she's doing and shut into a box and delivered to somebody as if she were merchandise.

Witches are only human, you know, even the most angelic of us. We want to be courted like real ladies, not pushed around like antique tarts."

"I understand all that now," Westfall said. "But now it is too late."

"Not necessarily," Ylith said, and her voice dripped honey.

"Really?" Westfall said.

"Open the lid, Westfall. I won't hurt you. I promise on my word as an angel. Let's see how we get along."

Westfall took a deep breath and opened the lid.

Ylith came out smoking, doing her witch's impersonation of Hecate.

Westfall screamed, "You promised not to hurt me!"

The chambers were suddenly quite empty. Westfall was in a dark corner of Limbo, and Ylith had taken to the air to report back to Michael. Pandora's box was still open and glistening faintly.

Chapter 2

Azzie arrived at Aretino's door one week to the minute after he had first talked with him. Aretino welcomed the demon to his home and led him to an upper sitting room where they could take their ease on brocaded chairs and enjoy the spectacle of the lights of Venice outlining the canals. Aretino served a wine he had chosen carefully for the occasion. A servant brought in little cakes for refreshment.

A soft blue twilight lay across the city, increasing by a hundredfold its air of magic and mystery. From below came the sound of a boating song: "Ho for the life of a gondolier!" Man and demon listened to it in silence for a few moments.

Azzie was experiencing one of the finest times in his life. This was the first moment of the launching of a new enterprise. The next words he spoke would make a great change in many lives; he was about to experience his own importance as a prime mover. Azzie was to become one who shaped events rather than being shaped by them. Power, self-aggrandizement, that was what it was all about.

In Azzie's imagination the new project swelled into immediate completion. It almost seemed done immediately after it had been conceived. His vision of it was vague but grand.

It took him a moment to come back to himself and

realize that everything still remained to be accomplished. "I have experienced some impatience, my dear Aretino, waiting to hear what you might come up with. Or do you consider the matter of my play beyond your competence?"

"I think I'm the only man for the job," Aretino said boldly. "But you'll judge for yourself when I tell you the legend I would like to base the play upon."

"A legend? Oh, good!" Azzie said. "I love legends. Is it about anyone I know?"

"God is in my story, and Adam, and Lucifer."

"All old friends. Do proceed, Pietro."

Aretino settled back, and, taking a sip of wine to clear his throat, began talking. . . .

Adam was lying beside a brook in Eden when God came to him and said, "Adam, what have you been up to?"

"Me?" Adam sat up. "I've just been sitting here thinking good thoughts."

"I know you've been thinking good thoughts," God said. "I tune in on you every once in a while just to see how you're doing. That's personal God involvement at its finest. But what were you doing before those good thoughts?"

"I'm not sure."

"Try to remember. You were with Eve, weren't you?"

"Well, yeah, sure. That's all right, isn't it? I mean, she's my wife, you know."

"Nobody's trying to make anything of it, Adam. I'm just trying to establish a fact. You were talking with Eve, weren't you?"

"All right, I was. She was going on about something the birds told her. You know, God, just between you and me, for a grown woman she does go on a lot about birds."

"What else were you doing with Eve?"

"Just talking about birds. With her it's birds all the

time. Tell me frankly, do you think the lady is all there? I mean, is she normal? Of course I don't have anyone to compare her to because I've never met another lady. You didn't even give me a mother, not that I'm complaining. But still, talking about birds all the time, I mean, come on already."

"Eve happens to be very innocent," God said. "Nothing wrong in that, is there?"

"I guess not," Adam said.

"What's the matter? Have I offended you?"

"You? Offend me? Don't be silly. You're God, so how could you offend me?"

"What else did you do with Eve other than talk with her?"

Adam shook his head. "Frankly, you wouldn't want to know. I mean, where is it written that a man should talk dirty in front of his God?"

"I'm not talking about the sex thing," God said contemptuously.

"Look, if you know what I did and what I didn't do, why do you even bother asking me?"

"I'm trying to make a point," God said.

Adam added something in a voice so low that God had to ask him to speak up.

"I said that you shouldn't get so angry at me. After all, you made me in your image, so what do you expect?"

"Oh, that's what you think, is it? And you think that my creating you in my image excuses any sort of behavior on your part?"

"Well, I mean, after all, you—"

"I gave you everything, all of it, life, intelligence, good looks, a cute wife, imagination, good food, a mild climate, good taste in literary matters, skill at many sports, artistic aptitude, the ability to add and subtract, and quite a lot else.

I could have put you on the Earth with one finger and left you spending all your time counting up to one. Instead I gave you ten fingers and the ability to count all the way up to infinity. I did it all for you. All I asked was that you play with the stuff I gave you but leave alone the stuff I didn't want you to touch. Is that right or is that not right?"

"Yeah, it's right," Adam mumbled.

"All I said was, that tree over there, what we call the Tree of Life, see that apple on it? And you said you saw it. And I said to you, 'Just do me a favor, don't eat that apple, got it?' And you said, 'Sure, God, I've got it and it's no big deal.' But yesterday, with Eve, you were eating the forbidden apple, weren't you?"

"Apple?" Adam asked, with a puzzled tone.

"You know very well what apples are," God said. "They're round and red and they taste sweet, only you shouldn't know how they taste because I told you not to taste one."

"I never understood why we weren't supposed to eat it."

"I told you that, too," God said, "If you had bothered to listen. It would give you knowledge of Good and Evil. That's why you weren't supposed to eat it."

"What's so bad about knowledge of Good and Evil?" Adam asked.

"Hey, any kind of knowledge is wonderful," God said. "But you have to have some knowledge to be able to handle knowledge. I was bringing you and Eve along nice and slow to the point where you could eat of the fruit of the tree of knowledge without freaking out or thinking you knew everything. But she had to go tempt you with that apple, didn't she?"

"It was my own idea," Adam said. "Don't go blaming Eve. All she knows about is birds."

"But she put you up to it, didn't she?"

"Maybe she did. But so what? There's a rumor around here that you wouldn't be so angry if one of us did eat the apple."

"Where'd you hear that?"

"I don't remember," Adam said. "Birds and bees, maybe. But Eve and I had to taste the apple sometime or other. The law of dramatic necessity says you can't just leave a loaded apple on the mantel without using it sometime. Can't just stay in the Garden of Eden forever, can we?"

"No, you can't," God said. "As a matter of fact, you're leaving at once. And don't think you're coming back."

So God put Adam and Eve out of the Garden of Eden. He sent an angel with a flaming sword to do the job. And so it was that first man and first woman met first eviction officer. Adam and Eve took one long last look at the place that was home and then walked away. They'd live in a lot of places after that, but none of them would be home.

It was only when they were out of Eden that Adam noticed that Eve didn't have any clothes on.

"Holy cow!" Adam cried, staring at Eve. "You're stark naked!"

"So are you," Eve said.

They stared all they wanted to at each other's private parts. And then they burst out laughing. And so sexual humor was born.

When they had finished laughing at each other's private parts, Adam said, "I think maybe we'd better cover up the hardware. We've got too much hanging out, if you know what I mean."

"Funny we never noticed it before," Eve said.

"All you ever used to notice was birds," Adam said.

"I can't imagine why," Eve said.

"What's that up there ahead?" Adam asked.

Eve said slowly, "If I didn't know it was impossible I'd say it was other people."

"How can that be?" Adam said. "We're the only people."

"Not anymore," Eve told him. "You remember, we talked about this possibility."

"Of course," Adam said. "I remember now. We agreed that other people was a prerequisite to having an affair."

"You would remember that," Eve said.

"I just never thought He'd actually do it," Adam said. "I always thought He meant for us to be the only people."

God had moved fast. At the beginning they had been the only people. But they'd done something wrong. Disobeyed orders. And so God punished them by making other people. It was hard to know what He meant by it.

They walked until they came to a town, until they came to a certain house.

Adam asked the first person he saw, "What is the name of this town?"

"This," the man said, "is Next Best."

"That's an interesting name for a town," Adam said. "What does it mean?"

"It means that Eden's best, but no one can get back there, so we live in Next Best."

"How do you know about Eden?" Adam asked. "I never saw you there."

"Hey, you don't have to have actually lived there to know it was good."

Adam and Eve settled down in Next Best. They soon met their next-door neighbor, Gordon Lucifer, a devil who had set up the first law practice in town.

"We think we need a lawyer," Adam said to Lucifer one day. "We think we were unfairly expelled from Eden.

We never got an eviction notice, for one thing. We never had a proper hearing in a court of law. We were not represented by counsel."

"You've come to the right place," Lucifer said, leading them into his office. "To right all wrongs, that is the motto of the Forces of Dark, the firm I work for. Understand, I'm not claiming there's anything wrong with the Big Fellow. God mostly means well, but He's entirely too high-handed about this sort of thing. I think you've got a good case. I shall file a claim with Ananke, whose obscure judgments govern us all."

Ananke, the Faceless One, heard Lucifer's plea in her chamber of gray clouds, where the great casement window faced out on the ocean of time, and the winds of eternity blew the white curtains.

Ananke ruled that Adam had been evicted unfairly and should be allowed to return to Eden. Adam was elated, thanked everybody, told Eve to wait, and went off to regain Eden. He searched in vain for the way to his former Paradise, but couldn't even find the end of his nose; God had covered the area with a thick darkness. Adam called upon Gordon Lucifer and told him what had happened. Gordon shook his head and summoned his boss.

"Well, that's not really fair," Satan said. "He is begging the question. But I'll tell you what. Here are seven tall candlesticks with magical properties. Use them wisely and you can light your own way back to Paradise."

Adam set forth, carrying six of the candlesticks in a camel's skin on his back, and holding the seventh in front of him, where its unearthly blue-white light cut through the gloom with surrealistic precision. This light afforded Adam unparalleled views of the way ahead and he proceeded boldly.

After progressing for a distance, with his candle in its

noble holder dispelling the dark on all sides, Adam came to a low wall with ivy on it, a still pool of water nearby. It seemed to him that this was the place where he had napped and dreamed so often back in the days of Eden when life had been simple. He stopped and looked around, and at once his candle went out. "Drat!" said Adam, because he knew no stronger word than that, this being an age before the birth of true invective, and plucked a second candlestick out of his pack.

The candle lighted itself, and Adam went on again. This time when the darkness was dispelled he came to a glowing beach at twilight, with a little island in the distance, and warm air flowing smoothly over all of it. And again he stopped, and again darkness descended as the candle flame went out.

Time and time again this happened, God's darkness confusing Adam's mind, presenting him with places that seemed for a moment like his lost Paradise, but, upon extinguishing the candle, proved to be otherwise. When the final candle went out, Adam found himself back where he had started, and there, willy-nilly, he stayed.

After Adam's seventh failure, Ananke ruled that that was how it was going to be, and overruled her own previous judgment. She pointed out that despite her own decree, Adam could not be returned to Eden, because his expulsion marked the first turning of the wheel of dharma and his failure to get back despite the help of the seven candlesticks revealed some of the fundamental code of the possibilities of the universe. It seemed, Ananke pointed out, that the entire world of sentient beings was based on a mistake made at the beginning, when the code governing the karmic machinery was set forth. Adam could be considered the first victim of divine cause and effect.

Chapter 3

Thus Aretino finished his story, and he and Azzie sat in silence for a long time in the darkened room. Full night had come, and the candles had burned down to guttering stumps in the pewter holders. Presently Azzie stirred himself and said, "Where did you get it?"

Aretino shrugged. "Obscure gnostic fable."

"I've never heard of it, and demons are supposed to know more theological speculation than poets. Are you quite sure you didn't make it up yourself?"

"Would it matter if I had?" Aretino asked.

"Not one bit! Wherever the tale came from, I like it. Our play will be about seven pilgrims, and we will give each of them a golden candlestick, possession of which will grant each of them his heart's desire."

"Wait a minute," said Aretino. "I never said there were any golden candlesticks. Not really. It's a legend, that's all, and if there are any golden candlesticks I don't know if they have any power."

"That's a mere quibble," Azzie said. "I love the tale and we must have golden candlesticks for our retelling of the legend even if we have to make them ourselves. But perhaps they still exist somewhere. If so, I'll find them. If not, I'll come up with something."

"What about the people who will carry them? The people who are to act out the story?" Aretino said.

"I'll pick them myself," Azzie said. "I'll choose seven pilgrims, and give each a candlestick and a chance to get his heart's desire. All he—or she—has to do is take the candlestick; the rest will be done for him. Magically, as it were."

"What qualities will you look for in your pilgrims?" Aretino asked.

"Nothing special. I just need seven people who want a wish granted without difficulty. They shouldn't be hard to find."

"You're not going to insist that they win their heart's desires through perseverance and good character?"

"No. My play will prove the opposite of that sort of thing. It will show that any person can aspire to the highest Good without having to lift a finger to help himself."

"That's really unprecedented," Aretino said. "You're going to prove that luck and chance rule men's lives, rather than moral observances."

"That's what I intend," Azzie said. "That's the whole point of Evil: proving that the weaker case is best. What do you think of my moral, Aretino?"

Aretino shrugged. "Chance rules? It's the sort of reflection that weak men love."

"Good. It will win us a big audience."

"If that is what you want," Aretino said, "I have no objections to it. Whether I serve Bad or Good, everything I write is propaganda and special pleading. You are paying for this play, after all. I am merely the artist accepting the commission. If you want a play demonstrating that green gallstones bring May flowers, pay me and I'll write it for you. The big question is, do you like my idea?"

"I love it!" Azzie cried. "We must get started on it immediately."

Aretino said, "We'll need to consider what theater to use. That always makes a difference in the way I block out my scenes. Have you any particular actors and actresses in mind? If not, there are several I could recommend."

Azzie leaned back in his chair and laughed. Dancing flames from the nearby fireplace cast sharp shadows across his narrow fox face. He brushed back his orange hair and said, "I think I have not made my ideas clear to you, Pietro. What I plan is no ordinary play such as is put on in the porches of the churches or in places of public assembly. I'll have no hired actors mouth their lines and make a laughing-stock of my conception. No! I really will pick ordinary men and women for the job, people whose own desires and fears will lend verisimilitude to the parts they play. And rather than a raised stage with painted scenery, I'll give them the world itself to work out their dramas on. My seven pilgrims will act out the story as though they were living it, which of course they will be. The stories will tell what befalls each pilgrim after he gets the golden candlestick, and each tale will be different. Like the Decameron, you see, or the Canterbury Tales, but finer since it will be the product of your pen, my dear maestro." Aretino executed a small bow. "Our actors will act as if they were in real life," Azzie went on, "and they will not know that there is an audience watching, namely ourselves."

"Be assured I'll not tell them," Aretino said. He clapped his hands and his servant came in sleepily with a tray of stale petit fours. Azzie took one to be polite to his host, although he rarely used human food. He preferred such traditional Hellish dishes as candied rats' heads and thorax stew, or a human haunch nicely browned and served up with plenty of crackling. But this was Venice, not Hell, and he took what he got.

After refreshment, Aretino yawned and stretched and went to a nearby room to wash his face in a basin of water. When he returned he took half a dozen new candles out of a cupboard and set them alight. Azzie's eyes glowed in the dancing light, and his fur seemed charged with electricity. Aretino sat down opposite him again and said, "If your stage is the world, who will be the real audience? Where on Earth can you seat them?"

"My play will be for all time," Azzie told him. "My main audience isn't even alive yet. I create, Pietro, for the future generations who will be edified by our play. It is for them we labor."

Aretino was trying to be practical—no small trick for an Italian gentleman of the Renaissance. He sat forward, this big rumpled bear of a man with a large nose and high coloring, and said, "So I would not actually write the play?"

"No," Azzie told him, "the players will have to contrive their own lines. But you will be privy to all the actions and conversations, you will see and hear all their reactions to events, and from that you will weave a play that can be performed for future generations. The first time through, however, will belong to the world of legend, for this is how myth is formed."

"It is a noble conception," Aretino said. "Please do not think me critical if I confess that I perceive a difficulty or two."

"Name them!"

"I am assuming that our actors, no matter where they begin, will come at last to Venice bearing their candlesticks."

"That is how I visualize it," Azzie said. "First, I want to commission your tale of the seven candles as the basis for my tale." Azzie withdrew a small but heavy sack from his wallet and handed it to Aretino.

"I think you will find this sufficient for your start-up costs. There's more where this came from. All you have to do is write down the basic story line. You will not write the actual dialogue, remember. Our actors, whom I will choose, will do that for themselves. You will watch and listen to them, and be stage manager and coproducer with me. Later you will write your own play on this subject."

"I love the idea, my lord. But if you take a simulacrum of Venice and move it elsewhere in space and time, how will I get around to do what is necessary in the staging of our drama?"

"To that end," Azzie said, "through charms and talismans I will grant you the ability to move around freely in space and time for purposes of looking after our production."

"And what of Venice when we have finished?" Aretino asked.

"We will slip our sequestered Venice back into the time track of the real Venice, where it will fit as neatly as a shadow fits its object. From that point onward, our legend will cease to be merely a private affair, and will become a part of universal legendry, with its actions and consequences recorded in the annals of mankind."

"My lord, I love the opportunity this gives me as an artist. Not even Dante was granted such an opportunity."

"Then get to work," Azzie said, rising. "Write me out the legend of the golden candlesticks in a fair hand. I'll see you again soon. Meanwhile I've work to do."

And he disappeared.

Aretino blinked and passed his hand through the space where Azzie had been. There was nothing there but insubstantial air. But the bag of gold Azzie had paid him was solid and comforting.

PART FOUR

Chapter 1

Azzie was well content when he left Aretino's house, the memory of Adam's story still tingling in his mind, but he had become aware, with that fine demon's sense that he possessed, that something was curiously amiss.

The weather had continued fine. Little feathery clouds sailed across a sky of purest azure, like galleons of snow molded by children. All around him, Venice went on with its pleasures and its labors. Heavy-laden barges filled with clothing and foodstuffs sailed slowly across the Grand Canal, their bluff, gaily painted bows thrusting through the low chop. A funeral barge, all glossy black and silver, slipped silently past, its varnished coffin strapped to the bow, black-clad mourners standing silently together on the afterdeck. Church bells sounded out. Crowds hurried to and fro on the promenades, and nearby a fellow came past in motley, with coxcomb swaying and bells jingling, a comedian bound for an engagement at some theater, no doubt. A group of five nuns hurried by, the great white wings of their headdresses looking ready to loft them into flight. On a bollard near a line of tied-up gondolas, a large fellow dressed in white satin and wearing a broad hat sat with a sketchbook and colored chalks, trying to capture a likeness of the Canal.

Azzie walked over to him. "It seems we meet again."

Babriel looked up. His jaw dropped.

Azzie came around to study Babriel's sketch.

"Is it the view here that you're drawing?" he asked.

"Yes. Can't you tell?"

"I was having a little difficulty," Azzie admitted. "These lines here—"

Babriel nodded. "I know, I've gotten them wrong. This perspective matter is difficult to capture, but I thought I'd have a go at it."

Azzie squinted at it again. "It's really not bad for an amateur. I'm surprised to see you here. I thought you were going back to Heaven."

"And so I did. But Michael sent me back here to do some sketching and thus improve my understanding of European art. He sends his regards, by the way. And also inquired after the health of your friend, Aretino."

"How did you know about Aretino?"

"I saw you come out of his house. He's quite famous, of course, though most of his verses are scarcely fit for Heaven. He's notorious, too, isn't he? He was one of the Top Ten Sinners of 1523."

"Huh!" Azzie sneered. "Moralists are always prejudiced against writers who show life as it is rather than as they feel it ought to be. It happens I am a fan of Aretino. I merely went by to pay my compliments, nothing more."

Babriel stared at him. It had never occurred to him to inquire what Azzie was doing coming out of Aretino's house. But now that Azzie had called attention to it himself, the angel began to wonder. Although Michael had hinted that something untoward might be afoot, Babriel hadn't really given it much thought. Azzie was his friend, and, although he served Bad, Babriel couldn't really consider him bad.

It occurred to him for the first time that his friend

probably was up to something, and that it was up to him, Babriel, to discover what it was.

They parted with expressions of mutual esteem and a promise on both their parts to do lunch again soon. Then Azzie went off down the street. Babriel stared thoughtfully after him for a while, then returned to his drawing.

Babriel returned to his hotel in the early afternoon. The four-story building sagged down on itself and seemed squeezed in by the larger buildings on either side. Half a dozen angels were staying there because Signor Amazzi, the grim and reverent owner, made a special price for those associated with religion. Some said he knew that the quiet, well-mannered, regular-featured young people who came from some unspecified northern country to stay with him from time to time were angels. Others said he thought they were angles, repeating Pope Gregory's joke. Amazzi sat at his little desk when Babriel came in, and said to him, "There's someone waiting for you in the sitting room."

"A visitor! How nice!" said Babriel. He hurried in to see who it was.

The sitting room was cozy and small, a few feet below street level but illuminated by sunlight streaming through high narrow windows, giving it a churchly effect that the godly found pleasing. Michael the Archangel sat on a high-backed straw-seated chair off to one side, leafing through a papyrus travel brochure extolling the pleasures of upper Egypt. He closed it hastily and said, "Ah, there, Babriel! I just stopped by to see how you were getting on!"

"Oh, very well indeed, sir," Babriel said. He showed Michael his sketchbook, remarking, "I still haven't gotten on to this perspective trick, sir."

"Keep trying awhile longer," Michael said. "A working

knowledge of painting is useful in helping to evaluate the many masterworks Heaven has in its superlative collections. Have you encountered your friend Azzie again?"

"Indeed I have, sir. Just a little while ago I saw him coming out of the house of Pietro Aretino, the well-known scurrilous poet and ribald playwright."

"Did you indeed? What do you think it was all about? Simple fan worship?"

"That's what I'd like to believe," Babriel said. "However, a certain appearance of upset in my friend's behavior when I mentioned Aretino's name has led me to wonder if it might not be otherwise. But I hate to accuse anyone of possible double-dealing, sir, and least of all one who is my friend, despite being a demon."

"Your scruples do you credit," Michael said. "Though we would expect no less of one who is after all a full-fledged angel. But consider. Azzie, as a servitor of Bad, would not be doing his job if he were not up to some subterfuge conducive to the advancement of Evil in the world. So to accuse him of harboring wrongdoing is simply to give him his due. Of course he's up to no good! The question is, what is he doing?"

"As to that, I have not the slightest idea."

"Yet I think we need to find out. Azzie is no longer an insignificant personage. Twice has he served the Powers of Darkness in great affairs. There was the case of Prince Charming to begin with, and then the matter of Faust, the outcome of which is still under adjudication in the courts of Ananke. I understand Azzie now stands high in the councils of unrighteousness. It seems obvious that he is a prime player in those games that spring up from time to time to bedevil mankind and set the feet of humans on the path to damnation."

"My friend is as important as all that?" Babriel said, round-eyed with amazement.

"So it would seem these days," Michael said. "At the least, it seems wise to investigate what his interest is in the wily and too-clever-by-half Aretino."

"I think you're right, sir," Babriel said.

"And you, my lad, are the very angel to do it."

"Me? Oh, surely not, sir! You know how lacking I am in guile, your archangelship. If I attempted by duplicitous conversation to ascertain his purposes, Azzie would see through me in an instant."

"I know that," Michael said. "Your ingenuousness is legendary among us. But it can't be helped. You are in the perfect position to do a bit of spying, since you are here in Venice already. It should be easy enough for you to make the acquaintance of this Aretino. Go to him as one who has long admired his work, and speak to him, look around his house, see what you see. Even buy him lunch to draw him out further. We'll put down the cost to Heavenly Investigations."

"You really think it'll be morally okay if I spy on my friend?" Babriel inquired.

"It stands to reason that it is," Michael said. "One cannot betray an enemy, only a friend. Without betrayal there'd be no revelation."

Babriel nodded and agreed at once to do what Michael asked. Only later did he realize Michael had never given him a direct answer. By then it was too late to worry about it, though. While betraying a friend may or may not be a moral wrong, going against the order of an archangel is decidedly inadvisable.

Chapter
2

The next day, on the stroke of twelve, Babriel knocked at Aretino's door.

There was no response at first, although he could hear a variety of sounds from within. They seemed to be the strangest mixture of musical instruments and human voices, many of them raised in laughter. He knocked again. This time a servant opened it, a very proper-looking man save that his wig was askew. He looked as if he had been trying to do too many things at the same time.

"I wish to speak with Aretino," Babriel said.

"Oh, dear, everything is in such a state of upset," the servant said. "Wouldn't another time do?"

"No, it must be now," Babriel said with unaccustomed firmness, stiffened by the thought that he'd soon have to report his progress—or lack of it—to Michael.

The servant stepped back, admitting Babriel. He led the angel to a drawing room, and said, "Kindly wait here. I'll ask if the master can see you."

Babriel teetered back and forth on his heels, a trick he'd learned long ago to help pass the time. He looked about the room and saw a manuscript on a little drawing table nearby. He had seen only the words "Father Adam" when there was a bustle of noise and a group of people came in. Babriel sprang back guiltily.

They were musicians, but they had discarded their formal coats and jackets and were walking at ease in their shirtsleeves, playing their instruments. It wasn't any church air they were striking up, but rather a lively dance melody.

They passed through without so much as a glance at Babriel. They were intent on penetrating to some inner room from which a babble of voices and high-pitched squeals and brays of raucous laughter betrayed the fact that some mirthful activity was in progress. Babriel stole another look at the manuscript, and this time he was able to read a half sentence: "Father Adam, shortly after his expulsion from the Garden of Eden for eating the fruit of the tree of knowledge . . ." Then he was interrupted again, this time by peals of girlish laughter.

He looked up just as two damsels came running into the room. They were young beauties, one with dark tousled hair, the other with tangled blond tresses. They wore bright diaphanous clothing that floated behind them as they ran, one in playful pursuit of the other, and Babriel blushed as he became aware that their clothing was sufficiently disheveled to reveal carmine-tipped breasts and rosy thighs.

They stopped in front of him. In the most delightful French accent, the blonde said, "You there! Have you seen him?"

"To whom do you refer?"

"That naughty Pietro! He promised to dance with me and Fifi here."

"I haven't seen him," said Babriel, resisting the urge to cross himself because he thought the ladies might find it offensive.

"He must be around here somewhere," the blonde said. "Come, Fifi, let's hunt him down and punish him." She gave Babriel a certain look that sent a shiver down him from the crown of his head to the nethermost extremities of his toes. "Why don't you come, too?" she said to him.

"Oh, no, no," Babriel said. "I am supposed to wait here."

"And you always do what you're supposed to? How boring!"

Laughing, the girls swept on into the next room, down the corridor, and out of sight. Babriel mopped his brow and tried to get another look at the manuscript. This time he managed to read the title. *The Legend of the Seven Golden Candlesticks.* And then the sound of footsteps alerted him and he moved away from the table.

Aretino came in, his beard in disarray and his doublet unfastened, his hose hanging halfway down his shanks. His fine linen shirt was stained, probably with wine. He walked with a decided list to starboard, and his eyes were bloodshot and bleary, the eyes of a man who has seen too much too often but still seeks to see more. He carried a half-filled wine sack in his hand, and his step was none too steady.

With some difficulty, the poet came to a stop in front of Babriel, and with owlish dignity demanded, "Who the Hell are you?"

"A student," said Babriel. "A poor student from Germany. I've come here to Venice to bask in the bright sunshine of your genius, dear master, and to buy you lunch, if I may be so presumptuous. I am your greatest fan in all the country north of Aachen."

"Are you indeed?" said Aretino. "You like my stuff?"

" 'Like' is a paltry word, dear master, to express what I feel toward your oeuvre. Men call you the Divine Aretino, but even that is to damn your genius with faint praise."

Babriel was not a flatterer by nature, but he had been around enough, in both high circles and low, to know how to handle the lingo. He only hoped he wasn't laying it on too thick for credence. But Aretino, especially in his present state, found no expression of his talent too fulsome.

"You speak well, my boy. I'll say that for you." Aretino paused to suppress a hiccup. "I'd love to have lunch with you, but it'll have to be some other time. I'm right in the middle of a party now in celebration of my new commission. Where in Hell are my guests? Up in the bedrooms already, I'll warrant. But I'm not far behind!" And so saying he staggered toward the door.

"Might I inquire, dear master, as to the nature of your new commission? Your well-wishers all over Europe would be so interested to hear."

Aretino stopped, thought for a moment, then came back into the room and picked up the manuscript from the table. Tucking it under his arm, he said, "No, no! I am sworn to secrecy on this matter. But you and the rest of the world will be astonished, I promise that. The scale of the enterprise alone . . . But not another word." And so saying he walked out of the room, moving quite well save for the odd lurch or two.

Chapter 3

Rushing back to Heaven, Babriel went directly to the suburbs where Michael had his split-level ranch house. He burst in on the archangel in his study, a fine, well-lighted room where he had laid out his stamp collection on a rosewood table under a Tiffany lamp and was going over it with magnifying glass and tweezers. The blond angel's sudden appearance caused a gust of wind to arise, and the stamps danced merrily in the air. Babriel rescued a Capetown Triangular before it blew out the window, and he put a paperweight atop it to keep it safe.

"Terribly sorry," Babriel murmured.

"Just try to be a little less impetuous," Michael said. "You have no idea how difficult it is to get these rarer issues up from Earth without awkward questions being asked. I take it you've met with some success in your investigations?"

Babriel babbled about Aretino's manuscript, its title, its first line, together with the information that the poet was celebrating a new assignment, and, from the look of the celebration, a well-paying one.

"*Seven Golden Candlesticks,*" Michael mused. "It does not ring a bell. But come, let's consult the computer that the Heavenly Department of Attractive Heresies has recently installed."

He led Babriel down the hall to his workroom, where,

beside the Gothic file cabinets and the Romanesque desk, there was a computer terminal of the cubic design called modern. The archangel sat down at the console, clapped a pair of spectacles on the end of his nose, and typed in various identifying words. He did other things with the keys, and soon data was flowing, black and green, down the screen in a rushing stream. Babriel blinked, but it was all going by too rapidly for him. Michael seemed to have no difficulty scanning the information, however, and he soon nodded and looked up.

Objections had been raised as to the suitability of computers in Heaven. The main argument in their favor pointed out that they were mere extensions of quill pen and stone tablet, both sanctioned for use in portrayals of spiritual places for purposes of signifying the Idea of Information. The computer was inherently no different from earlier writing technologies, and it had the virtue of taking little room in which to store a lot of information—unlike stone tablets, which could grow quite unwieldy and brought with them the attendant need of reinforcing the floors of the places where they were stored. Even parchment papers, though light by comparison to stone tablets, had their problems, not least of which was their destructibility.

"What did the computer tell you?" Babriel asked.

"It seems there is an old gnostic legend about Satan giving Adam seven golden candlesticks with which to find his way back to Eden."

"Did he ever get there?" Babriel asked eagerly.

"Of course not!" Michael snapped. "Don't you think you'd have heard about it if he had? Don't you realize that all of mankind's history is based on the fact that Adam didn't get back to Eden, and that he and every other man are still striving for it?"

"Of course, sir. I didn't think."

"If the Enemy is playing around with a story from the earliest days of creation, when the ground rules were set up to run the interaction between men and spirits, that is a matter of considerable interest to us. Seven golden candlesticks!"

"Did they ever exist?" Babriel asked.

"Probably not."

"Then presumably they don't exist today and can do us no harm."

"Don't jump to conclusions," Michael said. "Myths are the damnedest things. If those candlesticks did exist, they could cause a lot of trouble in the wrong hands. The risk is so terrifying that I think we must assume they do exist until proven otherwise, and even then we must remain cautious."

"Yes, sir. But if Azzie had the candlesticks, what would he do with them?"

Michael shook his head. "That is still hidden from me. But it won't be for long. I am going to look into this matter personally."

"And what about me, sir?" Babriel asked. "Shall I get back to spying on Azzie?"

The archangel nodded. "You're getting the idea," Michael said.

Babriel hurried back to Venice. But a hurried search, and then a more careful search, convinced him that Azzie was no longer in that city.

Chapter
4

Azzie had been called to Hell in a peremptory fashion. His head was still spinning as he stood in Satan's sitting room in the white clapboard house where the CEO of Hell did much of his business.

A demon in blue suit and rep tie came out. "His Excellency will see you now." And just like that, Azzie was in the chambers of Satan. Satan's place looked like a Long Island sitting room in a fancy house in one of the best suburbs. There was nothing particularly Satanic about it—just golf trophies, hunting prints, and a smell of fine old leather.

Satan had all the elaborate Hellish stuff, the torture instruments, recordings of Black Masses, all the stage trappings, but they were in a different part of the house, which he kept for official business.

Satan was smallish, with neat, prissy features, balding, bespectacled. He could take on any appearance he pleased, but he generally favored an unassuming look; at the moment he wore a yellow dressing robe with a paisley ascot tied around the neck.

"Ah, Azzie, it's been a long time! I haven't seen you since you were in my class on the ethics of Evil, back in the good old university days."

"Those were the good old days, sir," Azzie said. He had always been impressed with Satan. Satan was one of the main architects and theoreticians of Evil, and he had been the demon's role model for many years.

"Now, then," Satan said, "what's this I hear about you putting on a play?"

"Oh, yes," Azzie said. "It's true." He thought Satan would be pleased with his initiative. Satan was always telling the young demons to get out there and do something bad.

Azzie said, "I got this idea for an immorality play from watching one of the other kind. You see, sir, our opponents are always trying to prove that good actions are the only way to get good results. That's propagandistic and quite untrue. My play is going to show how absurd their notion is."

Satan laughed, but there was something pained in his expression as he said, "Well, I wouldn't exactly say that! The opposite of Good is not exactly Bad. You will remember, I pointed this out in my classes on basic infernal logic."

"Yes, sir. I don't mean to put Bad in the position of meaning you don't have to do anything to be rewarded for it."

"I should hope not!" Satan said. "That's not the position that Good takes. That's a fact of life whether you're good or bad."

"Yes, sir," Azzie said. "I guess I didn't quite see it that way. I mean, can't I do a play that brings up some of the good features of Evil?"

"Certainly you can! But why did you use this rather tedious example? Why don't you show that Evil is clever and very chic?"

"Is it, sir? Yes, of course it is! I don't know, sir, I just got the idea that this would be a good thing to do. It's amusing, you see, and our opponents are so serious minded."

"Do you mean to imply that we here in Hell are not serious minded? I can assure you that's not the case."

"That's not what I meant, sir!"

"I'd be rather careful about this idea," Satan said. "I don't want to order you outright to drop it. Why don't you put it on hold for a while? I'll try to find you some other assignment."

"On hold, sir? I couldn't do that. I've already got people working on it," Azzie said. "I've made promises. I wouldn't want to stop my actors and go back on my word. Unless of course I am ordered to."

"Oh, no, no," Satan said, "I'm not going to order you to stop. Wouldn't that make me a laughingstock—if I ordered one of my own demons to stop putting on a play extolling Hellish activities! No, my dear fellow, it's entirely your choice. Just remember, if it doesn't work out the way you are rather fatuously hoping it will, well, you were warned. We did ask if you wouldn't like to at least postpone it until you could think it over."

Azzie was so shaken by all this that he left without asking after one of his main concerns: was the candlestick story really true? But he left determined to go on with his play, and to visit the one being he thought could help him with the matter, true or not.

Chapter
5

Azzie was determined now to find out whether or not the golden candlesticks actually existed. He had a plan either way: if they did exist, he would use them in the play he was going to stage for the edification of man and spirits; if not, he would find some craftsman who could make facsimiles.

But he was hoping they did exist.

Everyone in Hell knows that if you need an answer fast, you just go to The Man—Cornelius Agrippa, a figure of singular importance in recent centuries and still much discussed in the Renaissance. He lived in an ideal sphere that was neither spiritual nor material but had some odd makeup of its own that had not been defined yet. Agrippa himself had been surprised when it sprang into being, and he hadn't had time yet to assimilate it to his system.

The system was based on a statement so self-evident as to appear obvious, yet it gave curious difficulties when he tried to prove or apply it: the cosmos and everything in it existed as a unity; as above, so below, and all parts of everything were interdependent. From this it followed that any one part could influence any other part, and that the sign or symbol of anything could influence the actuality of the anything that it stood for, since they were equivalent in the unity that linked all things. So far, so good. The trouble lay in trying to prove it. Although Agrippa could influence many things with many other things, he hadn't succeeded yet in influencing all things whenever he wished. Furthermore, he hadn't yet accounted for the presence of chance, which occasionally seemed to throw all his calculations astray in a manner that seemed random, therefore illicit in a plan-built universe, therefore actually something else. It was that and similar problems that Agrippa attended to in his high-roofed old house in that space that existed neither in the material sphere nor in the spiritual.

"Azzie! How good to see you!" the archmagician cried. "Here, hold this for me, will you? I'm about to turn gold into a dark vapor."

"Is that really necessary?" Azzie asked, holding the retort that Agrippa handed him.

"It is, if you want to convert it back again."

"If that's what you want, why do it in the first place?" Azzie asked. The retort was starting to bubble in his hands, and the liquid inside had turned from transparent to ocher yellow shot through with green. "What is this?"

"A sovereign throat remedy," Agrippa said. He was somewhat smaller than middle height, with a full philosopher's beard and mustaches, and he even wore *payes* like the Hasidic rabbis he sometimes talked to at the tavern in Limbo where they met for refreshments and learned conversation. He wore a long cloak and a tall peaked hat with a pewter buckle on it.

"Why is an intellect like yours bothering to concoct throat medicine?" Azzie asked.

"I try to remain practical," said Agrippa. "As for the operation with the gold, I seek to reverse the process of melting it down to a black vapor and sludge, and so be able to convert any black vapor to gold."

"That would make for a lot of gold," said Azzie, thinking of all the sludge he had seen in his lifetime.

"So it would. But plenty of gold is what men want. And hermetism is above all a humanistic philosophy. Now then, what can I do for you?"

"Did you ever hear," Azzie asked him, "of the seven golden candlesticks that Satan gave to Adam to help him find his way back to the Garden of Eden?"

"It sounds familiar. Where's my owl?"

Upon hearing himself called, a large snowy white owl with speckled wings flew down silently from his perch up near the ceiling where the walls angled in sharply.

"Go fetch my scroll," Agrippa said. The owl circled the room once and flew out the window. Agrippa looked around puzzled, then his eye lighted on the retort in Azzie's hands.

"Ah, give it here!" He bent over it and sniffed. "Yes, that ought to do nicely. If it's not throat medicine, it'll do for the mange. I am very close to a universal panacea that will cure all diseases. Now, let's see that sludge."

He looked into his little furnace, where the gold had been bubbling. He frowned. "Even the sludge is now quite burned away. I could try to resurrect it from memory only, because the doctrine of universal correspondences posits no impossible conditions, and what the tongue can say the mind can conceive of and the hand can capture. But it's easier to start with fresh gold. Hello, here's my owl again."

The owl flew to his shoulder. In his beak he carried a large rolled parchment. Agrippa took it, and the owl returned to his overhead perch. Agrippa unrolled the scroll and read through it rapidly. "Aha!" he cried. "Here it is! The seven golden candlesticks do indeed exist. They are stored with all the other lost myths the world has known in the Cathar castle of Krak Herrenium."

"Where's that?" Azzie asked.

"In Limbo, due south from the zero meridian of Purgatory. Do you know how to get there?"

"No problem," said Azzie. "Thank you very much!" And he was off.

Chapter 6

Babriel kept a close watch for Azzie's return. The angel had found quarters close to Aretino's house—a small place, for he didn't need much. He also acquired a servant, an old woman with sunken mouth and bright black eyes round as buttons. She cooked for him, the gruel of the righteous, which Babriel preferred above all other victuals. She washed his paintbrushes when he came home from his experiments in perspective, and in all ways looked out for him.

Babriel might have missed Azzie's return to Venice, for the demon flashed down in the night like a thunderbolt and made straight for Aretino's house. But Agatha, as the old woman was called, had been keeping watch, and her whole family had been enlisted into the task. Her father, Menelaus, was the first to see the quickening of light in the western sky, and he went to tell Agatha. Lighting a candle, she went through the dark passages to where Babriel stayed, knocked on the door, and entered.

"The one you seek is here in Venice, master," she said.

"At last!" Babriel said. He wound a cloak around himself, as dark a one as he could find, and he went forth.

Deciding to use the quality of subterfuge that he had

heard so much about, Babriel climbed Aretino's trellis and came to rest on a small balcony outside a second-story window. Inside he could see Azzie and Aretino, but he could not make out their voices. Irritably he said, "Time for a miracle here," and with those words, a glowworm detached itself from its game of tag with its fellows and came over to him.

"How do you do, sir? What can I do for you?"

"I want to know what is being said inside."

"Trust me, I'm the lad to find it out."

The glowworm moved away, and after a while found a chink in the window frame. He buzzed in just in time to hear Azzie say, "I don't know what you have in mind, Aretino, but we'll try it. And we'll do it now!" And with that there was a flash of light and Azzie and Aretino disappeared.

The glowworm returned and told this to Babriel, who decided he had been messing with complicated matters, because he didn't understand at all what had happened.

Inside the house, just before the glowworm's arrival, Azzie had been saying, "I just dropped by to tell you I've found the candlesticks."

"You have? Where are they?"

"According to Cornelius Agrippa, they're stored in a castle in Limbo. I'll pop over there and make sure they're still available, and then set them up as prizes."

"Prizes?"

"Really, Pietro, get with it. You thought up the candlesticks. Or remembered the story, whichever it was. There are seven of them, so we will have seven pilgrims. All they have to do is get the candlesticks, and their dearest wishes will come true. How do you like that?"

"I like it fine," Aretino said. "It's what I've always wanted. To take something in my hand and wish on it and what I want comes true."

"And not because you did anything to deserve it, either," Azzie said. "Just because you possessed the magical object. That's how things ought to work. Sometimes that's how they do work. At least, that's what our play is going to say. I'm going to tell my volunteers that all they need to do is find the candlesticks and their problems are over. Basically."

Aretino raised his eyebrows, but nodded and also murmured, "Basically, yes. But how will they get the candlesticks?"

"I'll give the pilgrims each a spell, and the spell will lead them to the candlesticks."

"Sounds all right to me," Aretino said. "So we're going to Limbo. Is it very far?"

"Quite far, by any objective standard," Azzie said. "But the way we do it, it'll take very little time at all. As a playwright you should find this interesting, Pietro. No living man, to my knowledge, has been to Limbo—except Dante. You're sure you want to make the trip?"

"Wouldn't miss it for the world," Aretino said.

"Then we're off." Azzie made a sign, and the two of them vanished.

Aretino's first view of Limbo was disappointing. The place was all done up in shades of gray. In the foreground were rectangular blocks that might have been trees, on one of which Azzie stood. Or perhaps they stood for trees. It was hard to tell what stood for what in this place.

Behind them, triangular blobs, lighter in color and smaller, seemed to indicate mountains. Between the trees and the mountains were areas of crosshatching that might have been anything at all. There was no stir of wind. What little water there was lay in stagnant pools.

Presently a small dark blob on the horizon attracted Aretino's view. They moved in that direction. Bats squealed around them and little rodents hurried by.

Chapter 7

Above the door of castle Krak Herrenium was a sign that said ABANDON THE FANTASIES OF REASON, YE WHO ENTER HERE.

Soft music came from within the castle. The tune was lively, yet it had something of a dirge about it. Aretino wasn't exactly frightened—it is difficult for a poet to be frightened when he's walking with his demon. The demon is more scary than the world around him.

A man came through a low arched doorway, stooping to fit under. He was a large man, and tall. He wore a billowing cloak over his baldric and jacket; on his feet were peaked boots. He had a bold face with large and expressive eyes. Clean-shaven he was, and there was about his face a look of powerful subtlety.

The man stepped forward and bowed low. "I am Fatus. Who might you be?"

"So this is Fatus' castle," Aretino mused. "How fascinating!"

"I knew you'd like it," Azzie said, "what with your well-known reputation for seeking novelty."

"My taste for novelty extends itself more to people than to things," Aretino said.

Fatus' eyes twinkled as he said, "Good day to you, demon! I see you have brought a friend."

"This is Pietro Aretino," Azzie said. "He is a human."

"Delighted."

"We have come on a quest that I think you can help us with," Azzie said.

Fatus smiled and gestured. A small table and three chairs appeared. There was wine on the table, and a bowl of sweetmeats.

Fatus said, "Perhaps you would care to have a snack with me while we discuss it?"

Azzie nodded and sat down.

They munched and talked, and after a while Fatus made a gesture calling for entertainment. At his signal, a troupe of jugglers came out of a back room. These men were of the breed called legal manipulators, and they threw a circle of torts and reprisals into the air and passed them from hand to hand and up and down and in and out, and Azzie marveled greatly at their dexterity.

At length Fatus smiled and said, "So much for illusion. What may I do for you?"

"I have heard," Azzie said, "that you store many old and curious items here in your castle."

"That I do," Fatus said. "Eventually it all comes to me, and I find room for it, whatever it is. Usually it's dross, but sometimes it's the real thing. Sometimes these treasures are truly prophesied, sometimes the stories are without a shadow of truth to them. I don't care, I make no distinction between real and unreal, realized and unrealized, manifest and hidden. What treasure are you seeking?"

"Seven golden candlesticks," Azzie said, "given by Satan to Father Adam."

"I know the ones you are referring to. I have some pictures of them you could look at."

"I want only the real things," Azzie said.

"And what do you intend to do with these candlesticks once you have them?"

"My dear Fatus, I am beginning a great enterprise, and these candlesticks play a part in it. But perhaps you need them for some purpose of your own."

"Not at all," said Fatus. "I'd be delighted to loan them to you."

"What I had in mind," Azzie said, "is loaning these candlesticks to humans so that they could get their dearest wishes fulfilled."

"What a nice idea," Fatus said. "There really should be more of that in the world. How do you plan to carry this out?"

"With the aid of spells," Azzie said.

"Spells!" Fatus said. "What a good idea! Spells can make just about anything work."

"Yes," Azzie said. "That's the wonderful thing about them. Now, if you'll permit, Aretino and I will just collect those candlesticks and then go back to Earth and get the spells."

Chapter 8

Azzie hid the candlesticks in a cave near the Rhine, then continued to Venice where he dropped Aretino off at his home.

The next part of this, the procuring of the spells, was best done without human participation.

Azzie took off at once, using his season pass on the Secret Routes to Hell to get him a direct line through the firmament to the river Styx. The Secret Route dumped him in Grand Central Clearing Station, where all of Hell's destinations are exhibited on the Devil's own bulletin board, with flashing lights to show trains soon to depart. The long banks of trains, many of them steam driven, stretched as far as the eye could see. Each one had a conductor in front, looking impatiently at his watch while eating from his brown-bag lunch.

"Can I help, sir?"

Azzie had been approached by a professional guide of the sort that hangs around every great terminus. This fellow, a goblin with a cap pulled down over his forehead, pocketed Azzie's coins and took him to the right train.

Azzie had time to find the club car and have an espresso as the train pulled out of Hell Station and chuffed direct across the dry Badlands to the river country where Supply was located. In an hour or so they arrived.

There wasn't much to see. Supply was a flat and monotonous little town, with a scattering of honky-tonks and fast-food joints. Just beyond it lay Supply itself, the great complex on the banks of the Styx that provided the inhabitants of Hell with everything they needed to conduct their nefarious tasks.

Supply was made up of a series of stupendous warehouses, built on the always-popular super-Quonset model. The ground these warehouses stood upon sloped marshily down to the low muddy banks of the Styx. Culverts, ditches, and water causeways ran from these buildings down to the river. All of Hell's refuse poured directly into the Styx, without any treatment at all. This didn't pollute it; the Styx had been at maximum pollution since it was first brought into existence. Refuse and contaminants from other sources had the paradoxical effect of purifying the River of Hell.

Azzie found the building where spells were stored and applied directly to the clerk, a long-nosed goblin, who looked up from his comic book. "What kinda spells? What do you want to do with them?"

"I need spells to lead people to seven candlesticks."

"Sounds straightforward enough," said the clerk. "In what way were you planning on having the spells work? The simplest spell merely gives a direction, an address. It'll typically be a scrap of parchment or a shard of clay or an old scrap of leather on which will be the words, for example, 'Go straight to the crossroads, then turn right and walk until you reach the big owl.' That's a typical instruction from a spell."

Azzie shook his head. "I want the spells to bring my

people to the candlesticks, which will be hidden somewhere in the real world."

"The assumed real world, I think you mean," the clerk said. "Okay, you want a spell that doesn't just tell its recipient where to go, but also supplies the power to take him there."

"That's it," Azzie said.

"How much do your people know about spells?"

"Very little, I should think," Azzie said.

"I was afraid of that. Is the spell supposed to offer its holder any protection on his way to the candlesticks?"

"That would cost more, wouldn't it?"

"Of course."

"Then no, no protection. They've got to take some risk."

"So what we have now is a spell with built-in power that will indicate when the holder is on the right track by clicking or flashing or singing or something like that, and then I suppose will signal when he has reached the right place, the place where the candlestick is."

"Well, it should do more than signal," Azzie said. "I don't want there to be any doubt about their finding the candlesticks."

"In that case you're better off going with a half-spell operation."

"I don't think I know that one," Azzie said.

"Chaldean. A spell like that comes in two parts. The wizard—that's you—puts half the spell in a place the recipient wants to get to. A place of safety, say. Then let's say the recipient, the holder of the half spell, is in a battle. It grows very dangerous. He turns on the half spell and it spirits him away to where the other half spell is. This is the best way if you want to get someone out of somewhere fast."

"Sounds good to me," Azzie said. "I can put seven half spells near the candlesticks, and give the other half spells to my people, and when they invoke them, that'll get them there."

"Precisely. Now, do you also want a set of magic horses?"

"Magic horses? What on Earth would I want magic horses for? Are they necessary?"

"Not really, but if you're planning this for an audience the magic horses provide a spirited spectacle. They also add another layer of complication."

"Not too serious a complication, I hope?" Azzie asked. "I don't know how smart my contestants are going to be. But assuming they're like most humans . . ."

"Point taken," said the clerk. "The magic horses complication should be easy enough to manage. And it does add a lot of class."

"Put me down for seven magic horses," Azzie said.

"Right," said the clerk, scribbling on an order form. "Now, do you want the horses to have any real magical qualities?"

"Such as?"

"Well, extra puissance, nobility, comeliness, ability to fly, ability to talk, ability to metamorphose into another animal—"

"Those sound like expensive additions."

"You can have anything you want," the clerk said, "but you do have to pay for it."

"Make them magic horses then, but without any extra qualities," Azzie said. "That ought to be good enough."

"Fine. Are there any other complications you want to introduce between the receipt of the half spells and the arriving at the candlesticks?"

"No, if they just get that bit done, that'll be fine," Azzie said.

"Okay, what caliber spell?" the clerk said.

"Caliber? Since when did they come in calibers?"

"New ruling. All spells must be ordered by caliber."

"I don't know what caliber I need," Azzie said.

"Find out," the clerk said.

Azzie gave the clerk a bribe and said, "Each spell should be able to transport a human being from a location in one realm of discourse to a location in another. Then it needs to take him on to another destination."

"Then you need double-barreled spells rather than half spells," the clerk said. "Can't ask all that of an ordinary spell. There's a lot of energy required, changing realms of discourse. Let's see, how much do these humans weigh?"

"I don't know," Azzie said. "I haven't met them yet. Let's say a maximum of three hundred pounds each."

"The caliber is double if the spell has to move more than two hundred and fifty pounds."

"Make it two fifty, then. I'll make sure none of them weighs in above that."

"Okay," the clerk said. He found a scrap of paper and did some figuring. "Let's see if I've got this straight. You want seven double-barreled spells that'll each transport a two-hundred-fifty-pound human—and that includes anything he's carrying—to two different spots in two different realms of discourse. I'd say it'll take forty-five-caliber spells. Which brand do you want?"

"There are different brands?" Azzie said.

"Believe it," said the clerk. "Moronia Mark II is a good make. So's Idiota Magnifica 24. Makes no difference to me."

"Give me either."

"Hey, you've got to make the choice yourself. Do I gotta do everything for you?"

"Make them Idiota spells."

"We're out of Idiota spells. I expect some more in by next week."

"I'll take the Moronia spells, then."

"Okay. Fill in here and here. Sign here. Initial here. Initial to indicate you've initialed yourself. Okay. Here you go."

The clerk handed Azzie a small white package. Azzie opened it and examined its contents.

"They look like small silver keys," he said.

"That's because they're Moronias. The Idiotas look different."

"Will these work as well?"

"Some say better."

"Thanks!" Azzie cried, and he was gone. Back for the weary round back through Grand Central Clearing Station, and then to Earth again. But he was elated. He had what he needed. The legend. The story. The candlesticks. The spells. Now he just needed the people to act out his story. And that ought to be the fun part.

PART FIVE

Chapter
1

O n a brilliant morning in June, on an unpaved country road to the south of Paris, a coach and four came round a bend from behind a clump of majestic chestnut trees with a jingling of harness and a pounding of horses' hooves. Aside from the noises made by the horses, and by the creaking of the swaying coach, there was nothing to be heard but the hum of the cicadas and the loud cry of the coachman: "Gee up there, Holdfast!"

The coach was a big one, painted yellow and red, and it had two footmen on top behind the driver. There was a similar coach fifty feet behind it, and behind that, several horsemen moving along at a smart canter. A dozen mules were at the rear.

Inside the lead coach were six people. Two children—a good-looking young boy of nine or ten, and his sister, a girl-woman of fourteen with a head of crisp red curls and a pert expression on her comely face. The others were adults, wedged together uncomfortably but making the best of it.

The coach had begun to lurch badly. Had one of the following horsemen galloped up beside it, he would have seen that the right front wheel was making a curious looping movement. The coachman felt the change and pulled his horses back just as the wheel came off, and the coach came to rest on its axle.

The leading horseman, a corpulent, red-faced man, pulled up beside the window of the coach.

"Hallo! Everybody all right in there?"

"We're fine, sir," the boy said.

The horseman bent over and peered inside. He nodded to the adult passengers, but his eyes rested on Puss.

"I am Sir Oliver Denning of Tewkesbury," he told her.

"I am Miss Carlyle," she said, "and this is my brother, Quentin. Are you part of the pilgrimage, sir?"

"I am," the man said. "If all of you will get out of the coach, I'll have my man Watt see what he can do with that wheel." He jerked his head at Watt, a dark little Welshman.

"We are obliged to you, sir," said Puss.

"Not at all," said Sir Oliver. "We could have a bit of a picnic while Watt gets the wheel back on." His vague glance didn't quite include the other occupants of the coach.

Sir Oliver had noticed Puss even before the accident; probably when she had loosened her kerchief. The sight of her great head of red curls and her winsome expression had proven too much for him. Men, even proven warriors, got silly around Puss.

They found a sunny, grassy spot in a small clearing not far from the coach, and Sir Oliver unfolded a camp blanket that smelled not unpleasantly of horse. He was evidently an old campaigner, because he had victuals and even some utensils packed in a leather saddlebag.

"This is very nice indeed," Sir Oliver said, once they were settled down and he had a nicely roasted drumstick in his hand. "How often have I eaten like this during the recent wars in Italy, where I had the honor of serving with the renowned Sir John Hawkwood."

"Did you see much action, sir?" Quentin asked, more to be polite than any other reason, because he had decided that Sir Oliver spent most of his time around the quarter-master's wagon.

"Action? Oh, yes, a goodly amount," Sir Oliver said, and he spoke of a clash of arms outside of Pisa as though all the world should have heard of it. After that he alluded familiarly to other armed encounters in and around the Italian cities, which he termed desperate engagements. Quentin had cause to doubt this since he remembered his father telling him that most of the warfare in Italy consisted of bellicose public words and behind-the-scenes private negotiations, after which a city would fall or a siege be abandoned according to what had been agreed upon. He also remembered hearing that that wasn't true when the French were involved, but held for the most part in dealings between the Italians and the Free Companies. Sir Oliver never mentioned the French. Only the Colonnas and Borgias and Medicis and suchlike foreigners. Sir Oliver had some rousing tales of early-morning engagements in which small groups of warriors would engage similar groups with sword and lance. He spoke of midnight vigils in the south of Italy, where the Saracens still held sway, and told of sudden desperate encounters at little walled cities where death might drench you from above in the form of boiling oil and molten lead.

Sir Oliver was a short, thickset man, built like a block of wood. Middle-aged and balding, he had a habit of jerking his head emphatically as he made his point, and when he did that his little goatee waggled. He often punctuated his more dire pronouncements with a peremptory clearing of his throat. Puss, who was always up for any kind of mischief, had begun to imitate him, and Quentin was hard-pressed to restrain his laughter.

At length Watt came over and declared the wheel fixed. Sir Oliver said he was well pleased, and accepted everyone's thanks with manly modesty. He said that since they were all part of the pilgrimage to Venice, he expected to see a great deal of all of them, plainly assuming that the company of so handy and so distinguished a warrior would be to everyone's liking. Puss said in her gravest voice that everyone welcomed him not least because the company might have further need of his services if another wheel came off. Sir Oliver found nothing funny in this speech, but accepted it as his due, and didn't even wonder why Puss and Quentin and several other ladies fell simultaneously into a fit of coughing.

Later that day, the pilgrimage finally met the nun who was supposed to be traveling with them but who had not shown up at the point of rendezvous. She came riding up on a palfrey, with a servant following her on a mule and carrying her falcon. The coach stopped, there were hasty conferences, and room was made for her inside.

Mother Joanna was mother superior of an Ursuline convent near Gravelines, England. Her family name was Mortimer, and she made sure everyone knew she was closely related to the well-known Shropshire Mortimers. She had a large, broad face tanned by the sun, she carried a falcon wherever she went, and she lost no chance during the stops to take the bird out and loose the jesses and send it questing whenever any suitable prey was in sight. When it brought back some mouse or vole, all bloody and broken, she'd clap her hands and say, "Good score, Mistress Swiftly," for that was her name for the falcon. Quentin couldn't stand the way she talked to it, prattling on in her squeaky voice until he thought he'd burst into giggles. At last several members of the company prevailed on her to let the bird ride atop the coach with her servant. Mother Joanna sulked then until she saw a stag break cover at the edge of the forest. She tried to convince the other pilgrims to stop for an impromptu hunt, but they had no dogs along, except for somebody's little pug—and it would have been hard put to go up against a rat.

The company learned that Mother Joanna was not only a Mortimer but also the older sister of that Constance who had married the Marquis of St. Beaux, a brilliant match. But she herself, not wanting to marry, or as Puss whispered to Quentin later, not finding anyone who would have her despite her estates and her famous name, had prevailed on her father to settle her as head of a nunnery. She declared herself well pleased with the one at Gravelines, for the hunting thereabouts was second to none, and the nearby forest was also at her disposal. In addition, the nuns, she said, were of good families, and good dinner conversation was never lacking.

And so the long day passed.

Chapter 2

Sir Oliver leaned back in the saddle and looked about. They were still in open country. Pleasantly rounded little hills stretched on the left for many miles. On the right, a swift-moving stream sparkled. Ahead he could already see the outlying clumps of big trees that marked the start of the forest.

But there was something else, something that moved, a dot of red, coming down from the hills, coming down to intercept the road half a mile ahead of the pilgrimage train.

Mother Joanna rode up beside him on her well-trained bay. "What is the matter?" she asked. "Why have we stopped?"

Sir Oliver said, "I want to take a look at the territory before we plunge into it."

"What on Earth could you hope to see?" Joanna asked.

"I am looking for some sign of the bandits that are said to infest these parts," Oliver said.

"We already have our protection," Joanna said. "Those four crossbowmen who are feeding from our provisions."

"I don't entirely trust them," Oliver said. "Fellows like that are apt to run at the first sign of trouble. I want to see if the trouble presents itself first."

"That is ridiculous," Joanna said. "A thousand score bandits could be hiding just a few feet away in the greenwood and we'd never see them until they wanted us to."

"I'm taking a look anyway," Oliver said stubbornly. "There is someone up ahead."

Joanna peered at the road. Inclined to nearsightedness, it took her a while to identify the red dot as a man.

"Where did that fellow come from?" she asked, half to herself.

"I do not know," Sir Oliver said. "But he is coming toward us, so perhaps we shall learn."

They sat their horses in silence as the horseman approached. The pilgrim train was stretched out on the road behind them, the two coaches, four additional horses, and twelve mules, carrying the thirty people who made up the group. Some had joined them at Paris, where they had stopped only briefly for provisions. It was at Paris that they had picked up the four crossbowmen, pensioned off from the Italian wars, led by a sergeant named Patrice who had declared that he and his men were ready to hire out to protect the pilgrims on the perilous passage through banditridden southern France.

The pilgrims were not an entirely happy group. In Paris they had argued one entire evening about the route they would take to Venice. Some had been in favor of avoiding the mountains altogether and taking the easy way through the heart of France, but the English were making trouble again. Even if you were English, that route was to be avoided.

Most of the pilgrims had favored a more easterly route, through Burgundy and then down the western bank of the Rhône until they reached the dark forests of Languedoc, and came through them to Roussillon. This view had prevailed. Thus far there had been no incidents, but they stayed on their guard, for anything might happen in this accursed country.

The single horseman rode toward them at a smart trot. The fellow wore a scarlet doublet, and from his shoulders flowed a cloak of dark red fabric highlighted with threads of purple. He wore soft brown leather boots, and on his head a green felt cap from which floated a single eagle's feather. He rode up to them and pulled his horse to a stop.

"Good afternoon!" Azzie cried, introducing himself as Antonio Crespi, a Venetian. "I am a merchant of Venice," he said, "and I travel throughout Europe selling our fine Venetian cloth of gold, especially to merchants in the north. Allow me to show you some samples."

Azzie had prepared for this by obtaining samples from a real Venetian merchant whom he had sent home clothless but happy with his bag of red gold.

Sir Oliver inquired as to where Sir Antonio had come from, appearing as it seemed out of nowhere. Azzie told him he had taken a shortcut that had cut many miles off his trip. "I travel all the time between Venice and Paris, and it would be strange indeed if I didn't know the shortcuts and the safest routes."

Azzie smiled in his most affable way. "Sir, if it is not too bold of me to ask, I'd like to join your company. A single traveler alone takes his life in his hands in these parts. I could do your company some good, lending you the use of my sword if need be, and acting as a guide for some of the trickier parts of the journey yet to come. I have my own provisions, and would be no trouble to you at all."

Oliver looked at Joanna. "What do you think, Mother Joanna?"

She looked Azzie up and down. A hard, critical look. Azzie, who had been stared at by many, leaned back at ease, one hand on the rump of his horse. If they didn't take him on as a member of the pilgrimage, he was sure he'd come up with another scheme. Ingenuity at getting one's own way was one of the hallmarks of Hell.

"I see no objection," Joanna said at last.

They rode back to the wagons, and Oliver made the introductions. Azzie took up a position at the head of the column, his by right since he claimed knowledge of the country hereabouts. Sir Oliver rode with him for a while.

"What lies ahead in this immediate vicinity?" Oliver asked.

"There's deep woods for the next fifty or so miles," Azzie told him. "We'll have to camp in the forest tonight. There's been no bandit activity hereabouts for the last year or so, so we ought to be all right. By tomorrow evening we will reach the inn that serves this area. It's a first-rate place, maintained by some friars and boasting a more than adequate kitchen."

Both Oliver and Joanna were cheered by this news. It was comforting to know a good meal and a warm bed lay ahead. And Antonio was already proving himself an amusing companion. The young red-haired merchant had many stories to tell about life in Venice at the court of the Doge. Some of his stories were a little strange, and some were downright scurrilous, but that made them all the more amusing. Some had to do with the odd ways of demons and devils, who were said to visit Venice more than most places.

And so the long slow day passed. The sun crept across the sky, in no rush to complete its appointed rounds. Little white clouds moved like airy ships bound for the ports of the sunset. Breezes ruffled the treetops. The pilgrims moved at a walk, picking their way along the overgrown forest track, not hurrying because there was no rushing a day that crept along with the deliberation of eternity.

Utterly, preternaturally still was that forest. There was no sound except the jingle of the harnesses, and occasionally a crossbowman's voice raised in song. At last the sun reached its zenith and began its slow sleepy descent down the other side of the sky.

The caravan continued moving deeper and deeper into the great forest, where the brilliance of the day was dappled with green leafy shadows. The pilgrims in the coaches began nodding off to sleep, and those on horseback drooped over their reins. A doe ran in front of the foremost horses and disappeared with a soft explosion of brown and white and tan into the foliage on the far side of the track. Mother Joanna gave a start but couldn't summon the energy to give chase. All nature, as well as the people passing through it, seemed under the forest's mild enchantment.

Things continued in this way until evening was almost upon them. Then, finding a flat well-grassed little clearing, Azzie declared that it would be a good idea to stop here for the night, as the country ahead was more broken and difficult. The pilgrims were happy to follow his suggestion.

Footmen unhitched the horses and watered them at a little stream nearby. The pilgrims got out of the coaches; those who were riding dismounted and tied up their horses. The adults found or fixed up likely places to sleep for the night while the children, led by Puss, began a game of tag.

Azzie and Sir Oliver walked to the edge of the woods, where a fallen oak made a natural firebreak. They gathered twigs and branches, and then Oliver bent down and applied flint and tinder. He had never been particularly good at the job of fire making, but no one else seemed to be doing it and he didn't want to ask Sir Antonio.

The sparks flew into the dry tinder, but they snuffed out almost immediately. The Devil's own breeze ran along the forest floor, contrary to the usual way of things. Oliver tried again and again, but the malicious little wind blew out his efforts. He was having difficulty even getting the stone to strike. The harder he tried, the less effective he was. The breeze on the forest floor was acting almost as if it had a mind of its own: when Oliver finally got a little fire going, a sudden puff of wind from a different direction extinguished it.

He stood up swearing, trying to ease his aching knees. Azzie said, "Perhaps you will permit me to do that for you?"

"By all means," Oliver said, extending the flint.

Azzie waved it aside, rubbed the forefinger of his right hand with the palm of his left, then pointed his forefinger at the tinder. A small bolt of blue lightning flew from his finger to the tinder, remained there a moment, then went out. When it disappeared, a merry little flame was burning before them. No breeze blew it out. It was as if the wind knew its master.

Sir Oliver tried to speak, but no words came.

"Didn't mean to startle you," Azzie said. "Just a little trick I learned in the Orient."

He looked at Sir Oliver, and Oliver noticed tiny red flames dancing in his pupils.

Azzie turned and strolled back to the coaches.

Chapter 3

Azzie found Mother Joanna setting up the little tent she carried with her on pilgrimages. It was of bleached cotton dyed green, so it blended in nicely with the forest. It had bamboo staves to give it shape, and a variety of ropes with which to tie it down. Joanna was wrestling with the ropes now. During the trip they had gotten themselves into a tangle, and now they formed a mass the size of a goat's head—and just as obstinate.

"It's the Devil's own job, untangling this knot," she declared.

"Why, then, better let me have a go at it," Azzie said cheerfully.

She handed him the tangle of ropes. Azzie held up his left forefinger and blew on it; his forefinger turned a bright canary yellow, all except the fingernail, which extended itself into a steel-colored talon. Azzie tapped the knot with his talon, and a green nimbus of fire danced around it for a moment. When it died away, he tossed the bundle of ropes back to Mother Joanna. She tried to catch it, but the ropes flew apart before they reached her. She bent down and picked up the ropes that had just a moment ago been irrevocably tied into a knot to rival the Gordian.

"How on Earth . . ." she began.

"A fakir's trick, learned in an Oriental bazaar," Azzie said, grinning at her. She stared at him, and saw the tiny red flames dancing in his eyes. She was relieved when Azzie walked off, whistling.

Later that evening, the pilgrims were gathered around the fire; all were there except Azzie, who had declared his intention of taking a stroll in the woods to relax before bedtime. Oliver and Mother Joanna sat a little apart from the others; there was no doubt at all what they were going to talk about.

"The new fellow," Oliver said. "What do you think of him?"

"He fair puts the wind up me," the abbess said, reverting to an expression of her childhood nanny.

"Yes," Oliver agreed. "There's something uncanny about him, wouldn't you say?"

"Indeed I would. In fact, just an hour ago, I had a little encounter with him that has left me thinking."

"So did I!" said Sir Oliver. "When I had trouble starting the fire, Sir Antonio did it himself—with his forefinger."

"His forefinger and what else?" asked Joanna.

"Nothing else. He pointed it, and flames sprang up. He said it was an old fakir trick he learned in the Orient. But I say it looked like witchcraft."

Mother Joanna stared at him for a moment, then told of her experience with Azzie and the knot.

"It's not normal," Oliver said.

"No. It most certainly is not."

"And it's not some Oriental fakir's trick, either."

"That it is not," Mother Joanna said. "Furthermore, he has little red lights in his eyes. Did you notice that?"

"How could I overlook it?" Oliver said. "It is a devil mark, is it not?"

"That it is," Mother Joanna said. "I've read it in the *Handbook for Exorcising Demons.*"

Just then Azzie reappeared from the forest, whistling merrily. Over his shoulder he carried a young deer.

"I would be pleased if you'd let me provide tonight's dinner," Azzie said. "Perhaps one of your varlets could cut up this noble beast and roast him for us? I am going to take a bath in yonder brook. Running down a deer is sweaty work." And he took himself off, whistling as he went.

Chapter 4

The pilgrims were awake before first light. As the morning sun came filtering through the leaves, they packed, made a hasty breakfast, and were under way. All day they journeyed through the forest, keeping close watch for signs of trouble, but not encountering anything fiercer than mosquitoes.

By early evening Sir Oliver and Mother Joanna were peering anxiously ahead through the trees, searching for the first sign of the inn that Azzie had promised.

They were afraid he had deceived them. But he was as good as his word, and suddenly the inn lay dead ahead, a good-sized two-story building built of stone, with a supply of firewood stacked to one side and a yard for the animals and a shed for the retainers.

They were greeted at the door by Brother François, a large, burly, bearded man. He shook their hands as they trooped in one by one.

Azzie was the last to enter, and he gave Brother François a bag of silver coins, "To pay for our stay." He laughed and gave François a peculiar look; François staggered back as though struck by some unpleasant thought.

"Sir," the Dominican asked, "have I not made your acquaintance before?"

"You might have seen me in Venice," Azzie said.

"No, it was not Venice. It was in France, and it had something to do with bringing a man back to life."

Azzie remembered the incident, but he saw no reason to enlighten the monk about it. He shook his head politely.

After that, Brother François seemed upset and absent-minded. He explained about rooms and victuals to the pilgrims, but seemed scarcely able to keep his attention on his own words. He kept glancing at Azzie, muttering to himself, and when he thought no one was looking, making the sign of the cross.

When Azzie asked for the use of the little bedroom upstairs, Brother François was quick to agree, but seemed more thunderstruck than ever. He kept looking at the coins in his hand and shaking his head. At last he approached Oliver and Mother Joanna. "That fellow with you, that Antonio, have you known him long?"

"Not long at all," Oliver said. "Has he shortchanged you?"

"No, no. To the contrary."

"What do you mean?"

"He agreed to pay six centimes for use of the room, and he put the copper coins in my hand. Then he said, 'What the Hell, I might as well be generous,' and he pointed his finger at the coins. And the coins changed to silver."

"Silver!" cried Mother Joanna. "Are you sure?"

"Of course! Look for yourself." He held out a silver centime bit. All three of them stared at it as if it were the Devil himself.

Later Oliver and Mother Joanna went looking for François, to arrange their morning meal, but they couldn't find him. They finally found a note tacked to the pantry door. "Gentlefolks," it read, "please forgive me, but I remembered an urgent appointment I must keep with the abbot at the St. Bernard House. I pray that God will watch out for your souls."

"How very curious!" Oliver said. "Why, do you suppose?"

Mother Joanna's lips tightened. "The man was frightened out of his wits, that's why he ran away."

"But if he thinks Antonio is a demon, why did he not at least tell us?"

"I think he was afraid to say a word," Mother Joanna said, "since this demon has chosen to travel in our company." She thought for a moment. "We might well be apprehensive, too."

The soldier and the nun sat silently for a long time, staring gloomily into the flames. Sir Oliver poked at the coals, but he didn't like the faces he could see in the flames. Mother Joanna shuddered for no apparent reason, since no breeze had passed her by.

After a while she said, "We can't just let this situation continue."

"No, certainly not," Sir Oliver said.

"If he's a demon, we must take steps to protect ourselves."

"Ah! But how to find out?"

"We'll come right out and ask him," Mother Joanna said.

"Do so. I would be most grateful," said Sir Oliver.

"I mean, I think you should come right out with it. You are a soldier, after all. Address him to his face!"

"I wouldn't want to insult him," Sir Oliver said, after giving the matter some thought.

"This Antonio is not a human."

"Whatever he is, he might object to our knowing it, though," Sir Oliver said.

"Somebody has to speak to him."

"I suppose so."

"And if you're any sort of man . . ."

"Oh, I'll speak to him, all right."

"He is definitely a demon," Mother Joanna said firmly. "Those little red lights dancing in his eyes are a dead give-away. And did you notice his rump? It had more than the suggestion of a tail."

"A demon! Right here among us!" said Sir Oliver. "If that's the way it is, I suppose we should kill him. Or it."

"But could we kill a demon?" asked Mother Joanna. "It's supposed to be very difficult."

"Is it? I have no experience in these matters."

"I have but a little," Mother Joanna said. "It is not the duty of my branch of the Church to be engaged in turning away evil spirits. We usually leave that sort of thing to other orders. But one does hear stories."

"Which tell you . . ." the knight prompted.

"That killing a demon is apt to be difficult, nay, impossible," Mother Joanna said. "With the added embarrassment that, if you are able to kill it, it probably wasn't a demon at all, but some poor human with the bad luck to have red lights in his eyes."

"It seems to be a damned tricky position," Sir Oliver said. "What shall we do?"

"I suggest we warn the others, and then put together what religious relics we have among us and seek to exorcise the foul spirit."

"I don't suppose he'll like that," the knight said thoughtfully.

"It doesn't matter. It's our duty to try to exorcise demons."

"Yes, of course," said the knight. But he was ill at ease with the idea.

The other members of the party weren't surprised to

hear that Mother Joanna suspected a demon was traveling among them. It was the sort of thing one had to suspect in these unsettled times. There were reports of weeping statues, talking clouds, and more. It was well known that there were a Hellish great number of evil spirits, and that most of them spent most of their time on Earth, trying to tempt people. It was a wonder one didn't see demons a lot more often.

Chapter
5

They waited, but Azzie still didn't come down from his room on the inn's second floor. At last they voted to send Puss to invite him to come down and talk with them.

Puss knocked at the door of Azzie's room with less than her usual bravado.

Azzie opened the door. He was brilliantly dressed in a new long coat of red velvet with an emerald green waistcoat, and his hair was neatly brushed into a shining orange bush. He looked as if he had been waiting for an invitation.

"They want to talk to you," Puss said, pointing at the common room below.

"Good. I've been waiting for this," Azzie said.

He took a final brush at his hair, adjusted his coat, and came downstairs with Puss. The gentlefolk of the pilgrimage were all in the big taproom. The common sort hadn't been consulted, and were outside in the stables gnawing their crusts of bread and their herring heads.

Sir Oliver stood up, made a low bow, and said, "I hope you'll excuse us, sir, but we've been thinking, and, I should say, worrying. If you'd just reassure us, everything would be fine."

"What is the problem?" Azzie asked.

"Well, sir," Oliver said, "to get straight to it, you aren't by any chance a demon, sir, are you?"

"As a matter of fact," Azzie said, "I am."

A gasp arose from those assembled.

"That," said Oliver, "is not what I wanted to hear. You don't really mean it, do you? Please, just say it isn't so!"

"But it is so," Azzie said. "I showed you proofs earlier, just to get over and done with the tedious part of convincing you. Have I succeeded in doing so?"

"You have indeed, sir!" Oliver said, and Mother Joanna nodded.

"Fine," said Azzie. "Then we know where we stand."

"Thank you, sir. Now would you be so kind as to go away and leave us in peace to continue our holy pilgrimage?"

"Don't be silly," Azzie said. "I've gone to a lot of trouble to get this thing set up. I have an offer to make."

"Oh, my God!" Sir Oliver said. "A deal with the Devil!"

"Stop acting so," Azzie said. "Just hear me out. If you don't like my offer, you needn't take me up on it, and we're quits of each other."

"You really mean that?"

"On my honor as a Prince of Darkness." Azzie wasn't really a Prince of Darkness at all, but it did no harm to exaggerate a trifle among all these highborn gentlemen and ladies.

"I suppose it'll do no harm to hear you out," Sir Oliver said.

Chapter 6

Speaking in a loud, ringing voice, Azzie said, "Ladies and gentlemen, I am indeed a demon. But I hope no one will hold this against me. What, after all, is a demon? Merely a name for one who serves one of the two sides whose struggles govern all existence, human and superhuman. I refer, of course, to the principles of Good and Bad, Light and Dark, as they are called. Let me point out first the absolute necessity that there should be two sides to everything, for things are impossibly flat without that. I will point out also that these two sides should be locked in more or less equal struggle. For if only Good existed, as some seem to feel would be desirable, no one could make that moral effort toward self-improvement that is the very essence of human progress. There would be no contrast between things, no way to differentiate the greater from the lesser or the desirable from the reprehensible."

Azzie asked for some wine, cleared his throat, and went on.

"Having established the propriety of a contest between these two great qualities, it follows that one side cannot win all of the time. Otherwise, our contest is no contest at all. The outcome must remain in doubt, now one side showing the preponderance, now the other, and no final result may be discerned until the whole thing is nearly over. In this we follow a law as old as any, the law of dramaturgy, which gets its best effects from an equalizing of forces. Good is not even supposed to be that much more powerful than Bad, because once the issue is no longer in doubt, the contest is no longer interesting.

"If we can accept this, we can proceed to the next point which from it flows. If it is permissible for there to be a Dark to oppose Light, or a Bad to oppose Good, then those who serve one side or the other are not to be despised. We must not let partisanship cloud our reason! If Bad is necessary, then those who serve Bad cannot be considered superfluous, despicable, unlawful, inconsequential. I do not say that they need to be followed, but they should at least be heard.

"Next I'll point out that Bad, once you discount its bad press, has a lot going for it, in terms of sprightliness, if nothing else. That is to say, the principle of Bad, like that of Good, has an inherent desirability about it that men may choose of their own free will. To put it more simply still, Bad can be a whole lot of fun, and no one should feel bad about choosing it since it is as venerable and respectable a principle as Good.

"But will a person not be punished for having anything to do with Bad? My friends, that is mere propaganda on the part of Good, and not a true statement of the position at all. If it is all right for Bad to exist, then it must be all right to serve it."

Azzie took a sip of wine and looked at his audience. Yes, he had their attention.

"I am prepared now to get directly into my offer. Ladies and gentlemen, I am Azzie Elbub, a demon of some antiquity, and an entrepreneur from very far away. What I have come here to do, my friends, is to put on a play. I'd like seven volunteers. You'll find your tasks pleasant, and not at all onerous. As your reward, you will get to have whatever it is you most desire in the world. In fact, that's the whole point of my play: to demonstrate to the world that a person can have his or her dearest wish without having to do anything much to get it. Isn't that a nice moral? I really think it holds up hope for all of us, and is more indicative of the way things really work than the converse — having to work for something and to have certain qualities of character that will bring the desired thing into your orbit. In my play we prove that you don't have to be virtuous, or even particularly effective, to achieve reward. So think about it, ladies and gentlemen. Your souls, by the way, will not be in any jeopardy whatsoever.

"I am now going to retire to my room. Anybody who is interested can come and visit me during the night and I'll lay out the exact conditions. I look forward to discussing this more with you later, on an individual basis."

Azzie made a sweeping bow and went back upstairs. He had time for a light dinner of cheese and bread, and a glass of wine to finish it off. He poked up the fire in the grate and settled back.

He didn't have long to wait.

Chapter
7

Azzie sat in his room, half listening to the murmurs of the night while reading a fusty old manuscript of the sort that was always available on the shelves of Hell's more popular libraries. He loved the classics. Despite his gifts for innovation, which were responsible for his present adventure, Azzie was a traditionalist. There was a knock at the door.

"Come in," Azzie said.

The door opened and Sir Oliver entered. The knight was unarmored now, and appeared to have no weapon on his person. Perhaps he knew better than to go armed into the presence of a fiend from Hell.

"Hope I'm not disturbing you. . . ."

"No," Azzie said, "come on in. Take a chair. Glass of wine? What can I do for you?"

"I've come about that offer of yours. . . ."

"Intriguing, wasn't it?"

"Indeed. You said, unless I misheard you, that you could see to it that a man got his dearest wish."

"I did indeed say that."

"And you pointed out that he needed no special quality to get that wish."

"That's exactly the point," Azzie said. "For look you, if he had a special ability to begin with, what would he need with my help?"

"A point most excellently made," Oliver said.

"You are too kind. Now, how may I help you?"

"Well, sir, what I want most of all is to become known far and wide as a great soldier, the peer of my namesake, that Oliver who fought the rear guard for Roland back in the days of Charlemagne."

"Yes," Azzie said, "go on."

"I want to win a notable victory, against overwhelming odds and at no great risk to myself."

Azzie produced a small parchment pad and a stylus with a self-sharpening point. He wrote, "No risk to self."

"I want to be known to men far and wide, to be as renowned as Alexander or Julius Caesar. I want to be commander of a small company of very good men, peerless champions all, and what they lack in numbers they must more than make up for in sheer ferocity and skill."

"Ferocity and skill," Azzie noted, and underlined "ferocity" because it seemed a good thing to underline.

"I, of course," Oliver went on, "would be the finest fighter of them all. My skills would be matchless. I want to acquire those skills, my dear demon, but at no personal cost or hardship. I'd also like a pretty and compliant young lady, a princess if possible, to be my wife and bear my sons, and I would like to retire to my own kingdom, which someone would give me, free, and there I would live happily ever after. That last is important, by the way. I don't want any surprise endings making me bitter or sad."

Azzie wrote down "must live happily ever after," but didn't underline it.

"That's the general idea, sir," Oliver said. "Can you take care of all that?"

Azzie read over the list. "No risk to self. Ferocity and skill. Must live happily ever after."

He frowned over it. Then he looked up. "I can cover

some of your points, my dear Sir Oliver, but not all of them. Not that I'm not capable of it, of course, but simply because this play I'm putting on deals with others as well as you, and to take care of your points in their entirety would take a Heavenful of miracles and a Hellish amount of time. No, my dear sir, I'll find a way in which you can, without danger to yourself, win a notable victory and get rewarded richly for it and stand high in men's eyes. After that, you'll be on your own."

"Well," Sir Oliver said, "I was hoping for everything, but what you can do for me won't be a bad position to start from. If I begin as a rich and famous hero, I'm sure I can take care of everything else myself. I accept your offer, my dear demon! And let me tell you, I am nowhere as against the powers of Bad as so many of my fellows. I've often felt the Devil has quite a few points in his favor, and is no doubt a much jollier fellow to be with than his dour Opponent in Heaven."

"I appreciate your wish to please me," Azzie said. "But I'll hear no slander against our worthy Opponent. We qualities of Good and Bad work too closely together to wish to slander each other. Both Dark and Light have to live in the same cosmos, you understand."

"No offense meant," Sir Oliver said. "I have, of course, nothing against Good."

"No offense taken, at least none by me," Azzie said. "Shall we begin, then?"

"Yes, my lord. Do you wish me to sign my name to a parchment in blood?"

"That'll not be necessary," Azzie said. "You have signi-fied your assent, and it is so registered. As I explained, your soul is not forfeit for your participation."

"What do I do now?" Sir Oliver asked.

"Take this." Azzie reached into his cloak and removed

a small, intricately made silver key. Sir Oliver held it up to the light and wondered at its workmanship.

"What does it open, sir demon?"

"Nothing. It's a Moronia double-barreled spell. Put it away in a safe place. Continue your pilgrimage. At some moment—perhaps a few seconds from now, perhaps a few hours, but possibly even so much as several days ahead— you will hear the sound of a gong. That will be the sound the Moronia spell makes when it turns itself on to the Ready position. Then you must take the spell and urge it to join its other half. The thing is internally programmed to do that, of course, but it never does any harm to repeat the command. It will take you to its other half, which is located near a magic horse. The magic horse will have saddlebags, and in one of them you will find a golden candlestick. Am I clear so far?"

"Quite clear," Sir Oliver said. "Find candlestick."

"Then you must go to Venice—if you're not there already. Soon upon your arrival, maybe earlier, you'll find that your wish has been granted. There will be a ceremony with appropriate pomp when everyone has finished. You're released after that to enjoy your good fortunes."

"It sounds all right," Oliver said. "What's the catch?"

"Catch? There's no catch!"

"There's usually a catch in matters of this sort," Sir Oliver said dourly.

"How on Earth would you know what's usual in the matter of magical stories? Look, do you want to do this or not?"

"Oh, I'll do it, I'll do it," Sir Oliver said. "I'm just trying to be careful about what I'm getting into. But it seems, sir, if you'll pardon my saying so, a lot of fooling around. Why can't I go straight to the magical candlestick?"

"Because there are a few things you will need to do between the turning on of the spell and the final acclaiming of your great victory."

"These things—they won't be too difficult?" Sir Oliver asked.

"Now, look here." Azzie's tone was rough. "You'd better be ready to do whatever is required. If there's any doubt about that, give me back the key. It'll go very hard on you if you default."

"Oh, fear not," Sir Oliver said, holding up the key as though to reassure himself.

"As I said, you will receive further instructions."

"Can you give me a hint?"

"You'll have some decisions to make."

"Decisions? Oh, dear," said Sir Oliver. "I'm not entirely sure I like that. Well, never mind. I merely need to do what comes up and it'll all work out well for me, is that correct?"

"That's what I've been telling you," Azzie said. "Evil expects nothing more of a man save that he do his duty and try his best. More cannot be asked in the annals of Bad."

"That's fine," Sir Oliver said. "I'll be off then, eh?"

"Good night," Azzie said.

PART SIX

Chapter
1

After her release from Pandora's box, Ylith went to report to the Archangel Michael. She found him in his office in the Old All-Saints Building in West Heaven, where he was going over a great pile of parchment print-outs. It was late, and the other angels and archangels had left hours ago. But in Michael's office, the candles burned bright, for the archangel had been reading reports from his various operatives throughout the universe. What some of them had to tell disturbed him greatly.

He looked up when Ylith came in. "Hello there, my dear. Is anything the matter? You look a bit ruffled."

"As a matter of fact, sir, I've just had an adventure."

"Indeed? Please enlighten me."

"It was nothing, really. This silly man conjured me, and Hermes shut me up in Pandora's magic box, and I finally got free with the help of Zeus."

"Zeus, really? Is that old fellow still knocking around? I thought he was in the Afterglow."

"He was, sir, but he projected himself to me in the magic box."

"Oh, yes. I forgot the old gods can do that sort of thing. But what about the little angels whom you were taking around the English shrines? Is anyone staying with them?"

"As soon as I got free of Pandora's box I turned the

children over to the Blessed Damosel and came here to report to you."

"The Blessed Damosel didn't mind baby-sitting?"

"She was glad to leave off leaning on the gold bar of
Heaven for a while and do something practical. It's silly,
isn't it, sir, the way poems freeze us into postures we can't
get out of?"

Michael nodded, then said, "I have important work for
you back on Earth."

"That will be fine," Ylith told him. "I like visiting
shrines."

"Your work on this one will encompass something
more than sightseeing," Michael said. "It involves Azzie."

"Hah!" said Ylith.

"It seems your demonic friend is up to something
again. Something decidedly fishy."

"That's strange," Ylith said. "I saw him just recently in
York, and he had nothing more on his mind than attending
a morality play."

"That play seems to have given him some ideas," Michael said. "Now there are indications that he is attempting
something else. My observers bring me word that he has
involved Pietro Aretino, that scurrilous limb of Satan.
Given Azzie's already established proclivity toward the unexpected, I'm sure he's up to some mischief."

Ylith nodded. "But why should you concern yourself
with a mere play?"

"I suspect that it is rather more than 'mere,'" Michael
said. "Judging by Azzie's previous excursions, notably the
matters of Prince Charming and Johann Faust, this new
attempt, whatever it is, could bring the forces of Dark and
Light once again into direct conflict, and so involve us all in
another do-or-die situation. Just when it seemed we could
have some peace in the cosmos! These are only rumors,

mind you, yet we must give them some credence, put forth as they are by the turncoats we keep in the midst of the Forces of Bad to observe the enemy and tell us what they are up to. Ylith, I need you to do a bit of looking around."

"By 'looking around' I suppose you mean spying," said Ylith. "And to whom does 'us' refer?"

"Me and God," Michael said. "I'm asking you in His name, of course."

"Yes, you usually do," Ylith said. Her face took on a petulant expression. "Why doesn't He ever speak to me Himself?"

"Many of us have wondered why we do not hear direct from the Deity," Michael said. "He doesn't speak directly to me, either. It is a mystery and we are not supposed to question it."

"Why not?" Ylith asked.

"Some matters you must take on faith. What we must do is discover what Azzie is up to. Go and look over his pilgrimage, making up any excuse you wish to explain why you are there, and see what he is really about. Unless I miss my guess, our proud young demon won't be able to conceal his purposes from you because his project, whatever it is, should be in full swing."

"Very well, then, sir, I'll go at once."

"Do so. And use your own judgment. If you should find that Azzie Elbub has a scheme underfoot for the subversion of mankind and the glorification of Evil, it will do no harm at all to put a spike in his wheels, so to speak, if you should find a chance."

"That's exactly what I was thinking," Ylith said.

Chapter 2

In their room near the kitchen, Puss and Quentin lay in their truckle beds watching the shadows cross and re-cross on the ceiling.

"Do you think Antonio is really a demon?" asked Quentin, who was quite young and not completely sure yet what was real and what was not.

"I think he is," Puss said.

Puss had been thinking long and hard about what she wanted more than anything else in the world. The first thing that had occurred to her was blond hair, like her brother's. Silky and curly and long, and with a flaxen tint to it, not the brassy yellow that some girls affected. But was that really a thing to wish for above all else? Puss felt a little ashamed for having so meager a wish, and so, uncustomarily, she listened attentively as Quentin told her what he'd ask for if he went to ask a favor of the demon.

"My own horse, that's first," Quentin said decisively. "And my own sword. It's ridiculous of Father to say it's too expensive having a sword made for me because I'll outgrow it in a year or two. I mean, what's the sense of being rich if you can't buy things you will outgrow?"

"Very sensible," said Puss. "A sword, then. What else do you want?"

"I don't think I want a kingdom," Quentin said thoughtfully. "I'd have to stay around and take care of it. I don't think King Arthur was too happy despite being in charge of Camelot, do you?"

"I doubt it," Puss said.

"I'd like to go out on a lot of quests," Quentin said.

"Like Lancelot? He wasn't very happy, either."

"No, but that's because he was silly, falling in love with the queen when there were so many other ladies to choose from. Why choose any at all? I'd rather be like Gawaine, traveling around and having different girlfriends and getting into trouble, and winning treasures and then losing them again. That way he had the pleasure of getting stuff without having to take care of it later."

"Like getting all the toys he wanted without ever having to put them away?" Puss asked.

"Exactly," said Quentin.

"Very sound," Puss said. "What else would you want?"

"A magical animal for a pet," Quentin answered without hesitation. "A lion, I should think, who listens only to me and kills people I don't like."

"Well, that's a little much, isn't it?" Puss asked.

"I mean he would kill people I didn't like if I let him. But I wouldn't, of course. If they got too troublesome, I'd kill them myself, in a long duel in which I got grievous wounds. And Mother would bind them up for me."

"Mothers don't bind the wounds of heroes," Puss pointed out.

"They could if it's my adventure," Quentin said. "I could make a rule."

"It's a pity you're too young to make deals with demons."

"I don't know about that," Quentin said. He sat upright in bed and looked very serious. "I've half a mind to go visit him right now."

"Quentin! You wouldn't!" Puss said, thinking that if Quentin insisted, it would be her duty as his older sister to accompany him and perhaps make a wish of her own, just to keep him company. Quentin got out of bed and started to put on his clothes. His lower lip trembled as he contemplated his own daring, but his mind seemed to be made up.

Just then there was a flash of light in a corner of the room. Both children jumped back into bed. There was a great deal of smoke, and when it cleared a pretty, dark-haired young woman was standing there.

"How did you do that?" Quentin asked. "I don't remember you from the pilgrimage!"

"I came to sell my eggs to the pilgrims," the woman said. "I live on a nearby farm and just arrived here at the inn. My name is Ylith."

The children introduced themselves. They were especially eager to tell of what Antonio had said that evening, about granting the wishes of seven lucky people. Ylith recognized Azzie in the description.

"I want to go make a wish, too," Quentin said.

"You'll do no such thing," Ylith said firmly.

Quentin seemed more than a little relieved. But he asked, "Why can't I?"

"Because it isn't seemly for well-raised children to ask wishes of a demon from Hell."

"But other people are asking," Puss pointed out. "They're going to have all the fun."

"I think you will find that isn't really so," Ylith said. "Some of those people are going to find themselves involved in more than they bargained for."

"How can you know that?" Puss asked.

"I just know," Ylith said. "Now, children, how about trying to get to sleep? I'll tell you a story if you do."

Chapter 3

Ylith told a story about lambs and kids gamboling on the hillsides of her native Greece. Soon the children were asleep, so she tucked them up and blew out the candle, then sneaked out of their room. She found several of the pilgrims in the common room, sitting at a table near the fire and talking over the affairs of the day.

"Is it certain he's a demon, then?" one of the female servitors was asking a shock-headed fellow who was valet to Sir Oliver.

"What else could he be?" the valet replied. His name was Morton Kornglow and he was twenty-two years old, a rangy young fellow with ideas beyond his station.

Ylith sat down beside the woman and the valet. "What is this demon offering?" she asked.

Kornglow said, "My master told me he has to do a magical passage in order to be rewarded with his dearest wish. When I went to his room, he was gone. Vanished."

"Maybe he's just outside, walking around," Ylith suggested.

"We'd have seen him come downstairs," Kornglow said, "and he's unlikely to have dived from the window into the bramble below. He's off doing the demon's work, I tell you, and frankly, it sounds like work that would suit me."

"You wouldn't!" the female servitor said with an admiring glance.

"I'm thinking about it," Kornglow said. "I can be in the demon's play as well as any man, as long as it doesn't matter that I don't have a Sir before my name."

Ylith stared at him. "A play?"

Kornglow nodded. "That's what Sir Oliver told me. The demon is putting on some sort of play. We just have to do whatever it is we usually do, and we'll be rewarded greatly for it. That's the sort of life I want to lead."

Ylith got to her feet. "You must excuse me. I need to see someone."

She hurried off, went to the front door, and passed through it into the darkness.

"Where do you think she's gone to?" the female servitor asked.

Kornglow shrugged and sucked his teeth. "If she has an appointment it must be with an angel or a devil. There's nothing else out there but wolves."

Ylith said to herself, "So, he's going to do it! Stage an immorality play! Wait until Michael hears about this!"

Chapter
4

"Mounting an immorality play?" Michael said.

"So it would seem, sir."

"The effrontery!"

"Yes, sir."

"Go back there and keep an eye on his progress. If you should find a way ever so subtly to impede his plan, it wouldn't be amiss to do it. Nothing blatant, you understand."

"I understand," Ylith said.

"Then off with you," Michael said. "I may send Babriel down, also, to lend a hand."

"That would be nice," Ylith said, a little wistfully. Although she and Babriel were not currently keeping company, she still had good memories of their association. Ylith remembered very well what sinning was like, and at times her whole body ached for the good old days.

Memories of her affair with Azzie also came to mind. It had been what she had once considered great fun.

She shook her head, willing herself not to think so much. It could get her into trouble.

Chapter 5

After dismissing Kornglow, Sir Oliver sat for a long time on the edge of the bed, thinking of the bold thing he had done. He was frightened, of course; what man would not be frightened after having such a conversation with a demon? And yet Sir Antonio's offer was just too good to pass up. Despite the churchmen's complaints that the Dark Forces were always out trying to seduce mankind, it actually happened quite rarely. Never to anyone of Sir Oliver's acquaintanceship, and certainly not to him.

Oliver liked the idea. A great passion had burned in him since childhood—to get something big and valuable and important at the least pains possible to himself. It was not the sort of thing you talked to people about much. They didn't understand.

Although it was very late, he was not particularly sleepy. He poured himself a glass of wine and found a few biscuits he had secreted from the dinner for a late-night snack. He was just taking a biscuit out of his pocket when his gaze happened to fall on the wall to his right.

He gulped hastily, spilling wine down the front of his doublet. He was looking at a door in the wall. A common, ordinary door. But Sir Oliver was certain one had not existed there before.

He got up, went over, and examined it. Could he have

overlooked it when he first came in? There was a knob. He tried it. The door was locked.

Well, that was all right, then. He sat down again. And then another thought came to him, and he took Azzie's Moronia spell in the form of the silver key out of his pocket and walked up to the door again.

He pushed the key cautiously into the keyhole. It slid in with an unctuous click.

He put the slightest pressure on the key, toward the left, just to see what would happen. The key turned as though by itself, and the lock clicked back.

Oliver reached out and turned the handle. The door opened. He removed the key and put it in his pocket.

He peeked through. Behind the door was a long, dimly lit passageway that seemed to extend for a great distance, losing itself at last in gloom. Sir Oliver knew this passageway didn't lead to anyplace in the inn, or even in the forest outside. It led to God knew where, and he was expected to go in.

Frightening . . .

But think of the reward!

A momentary vision flared before him. It was himself, dressed in red armor, astride a mighty charger, at the head of a company of heroes, entering a city and being acclaimed by all and sundry!

"That would really be something!" Sir Oliver said aloud.

He stepped into the passageway, not really ready to commit himself but more in the spirit of a boy putting his toe into what might be very cold water.

As he stepped in, the door to his room at the inn closed behind him.

Sir Oliver gulped, but he didn't try to retreat. Some

faint presentiment had told him something like this was likely to happen. How else did adventures start but that something gives you a push and then there you are, committed?

He began to walk down the passageway, very cautiously at first and then with growing energy.

Chapter
6

There was enough light to see by, though Oliver was unable to make out how it was produced. It was an even gray light, like twilight, and it was a sad light, almost an ominous light. He kept on walking, and the passageway seemed to stretch on and on. Thin, leafy branches hung from the walls on both sides; they gave a pleasing rural effect.

He continued walking. The floor beneath his feet changed slowly into a real forest floor, and a natural luminescence lighted his way. He couldn't see far ahead, however, as there were leafy branches everywhere.

After a while the tree cover became thinner, and he came out into a grassy meadow. At the end of that meadow was a small castle, situated on its own little island, with a moat and drawbridge. The drawbridge was down.

He entered the grounds of the inner keep and saw a door before him. It swung open as he approached. Inside was a nicely laid out living room with a fire burning merrily in the fireplace. A lady was sitting on a small stool to one side of the doorway; she rose to her feet and turned to him.

"Welcome, sir knight," she said. "I am Alwyn, with a y, and I bid thee welcome. My husband is away killing people, but the hospitality of my house demands that I ask you to stay for dinner, and then to offer you a bed to sleep in, and finally, breakfast in the morning."

"Sounds good to me," Oliver said. "What I'd really like to know, though, you don't happen to be holding a magic horse for me, do you?"

"A magic horse? What color magic horse?"

"Well, that's it, you see, I don't really know. I was told there was a magic horse just ahead for me, and it would lead me to a golden candlestick. After that . . . Actually, I'm a little unclear as to just exactly what is to happen after that. I believe I am to be lord of a large body of armed men. You wouldn't know anything about that, would you?"

"No," Alwyn said. "I really have a very small part in this thing."

She smiled. Her dark hair was lovely and tousled, her breasts high and well rounded. Oliver followed her inside.

They passed through several rooms, all decorated in scarlet and black and silver and containing armorial bearings, arms, and dark portraits of stern-looking elders. In each fireplace a fire sparked and glowed gaily. They walked through six rooms altogether. In the seventh a table was set with a gleaming white cloth and silver service.

"Oh, I say, this is rather decent!" Sir Oliver said, rubbing his hands together. There were wonderful-looking foods before him, goose pâté and gooseberry jam, eggs and seed bread, and a great variety of drinks. The table was set for two, and Oliver began to wonder if the table were not the only thing that had been set up for him.

"Do take a seat," Alwyn said. "Make yourself comfortable."

A white kitten came under the archway and pranced and danced its way into the room. Alwyn gave a merry little laugh and bent to play with it. As she did so, Oliver seized the opportunity and exchanged plates with her. The two plates were almost identical, the only difference being that his had two radishes on the side and hers but one. He quickly placed one of his radishes on her plate to disguise his substitution. When she straightened up, Alwyn appeared to have noticed nothing.

They ate, and Alwyn poured two glasses of Burgundy from a great bottle on the damask-covered table.

Oliver found a moment when Alwyn's attention was taken up by a small foxhound that came into the room with a definite gamboling motion. Seizing the moment, he switched glasses. She didn't notice a thing.

Congratulating himself, he now turned to his assault on the provender, his favorite sort of a battle by far. He ate greedily and drank deeply, for the food was of a luscious perfection. This was fantasy food, magic food, just nothing in the world like it. Soon he felt the unmistakable sensation of some opiatelike drug attacking his sensorium and making him dizzy and faint.

"Is anything wrong, sir knight?" Alwyn asked as he slumped low in his seat.

"Merely a moment of fatigue," Oliver said.

"You've switched plates!" Alwyn said, staring at the knight's grimy thumbprint on her plate—proof enough of what he'd wished concealed.

"No offense intended," Oliver said sleepily. "Old custom of my people. You take this stuff on purpose?"

"Of course. Without my sleeping potion, I have a devil of a time dropping off at night," Alwyn said.

"Damned sorry I took it," Sir Oliver said through rubbery lips and eyes that seemed already to be rolling back into his head to reveal that passage into dreams that he would rather not take. "How long before it wears off?"

Her reply was lost in a crashing wave of sleep that broke over Oliver's head. He struggled in it like a man caught in raging surf; then he was out of the surf and falling deep into the black pool that lapped around him like a warm bath. He struggled to keep his head above the soapy marble waves sent by Morpheus. He wrestled with strange thoughts, unaccountable insights. And then, before he even knew it, he was gone.

When he came to again, the woman was gone. The castle was gone. He was in a different place entirely.

Chapter 7

When Ylith returned to the pilgrimage, she found all in a state of confusion. Sir Oliver had vanished suddenly during the night, leaving no trail. His valet, Morton Kornglow, was at a loss to explain his disappearance except through magic.

Ylith looked around the area and finally went to the room Sir Oliver had occupied. The faint smell of prussic acid could be taken almost as proof positive that a Moronia spell had been used here within the last twenty-four hours.

That was all Ylith needed. She waited until she was alone in Oliver's room, then quickly performed her own enchantment. She used ingredients she always carried in her witches' kit—a thing she had never abandoned, despite her conversion—and soon, taking on a vaporous form, she was off and away, passing through the great forest into which Oliver had disappeared.

Presently she came across the knight's trail and followed it to Alwyn's castle. Ylith knew Alwyn slightly from the old days. Alwyn was another witch, of the old, unreformed kind, and Ylith knew she was probably doing a job for Azzie.

It was time to scry out the immediate future. She had gathered enough evidence to direct the scrying instruments; now she set them to motion.

The results were as she had hoped. Sir Oliver was currently going through an adventure with Alwyn. Azzie had set it up as simple enough to get through fairly quickly; afterward, Sir Oliver would have a longish walk. Then he would be out of the forest and on his way to his goal, which lay on the southern slope of the Alps in Italian territory.

The logical place to interrupt him was somewhere before he emerged from the forest. She could intercept his path. But what then? She needed a way to stop him, but a way to do that without harming him.

"I've got it!" she said. She packed up her scrying equipment and conjured an afreet of her acquaintance.

The afreet soon appeared, large and black and with an ill-tempered look. Ylith explained briefly what was going on, and how Sir Oliver had to be stopped or delayed.

"He must be stopped," Ylith said to the afreet.

"I'll be happy to oblige," said the formerly evil being who had recently converted to the side of Good. "Shall I strike him dead?"

Creatures like this still had a certain propensity toward violence, which was looked down upon in quieter times when a certain liberalism was allowed to reign in Heaven. But this was not a quiet time, and the feelings of the intellectuals in Heaven could no longer be worried about.

"No, that's going too far," Ylith said. "But do you know that roll of invisible fencing we took from Baal's magicians some years ago?"

"Yes, madam. It was declared an anomaly and stored in one of the warehouses."

"Find out which warehouse and get yourself a good-sized piece of it. Here is what I want you to do with it."

Chapter
8

Oliver sat up slowly and said to himself, "Wow, what was that all about?" He clutched his head where a precursor to a migraine was tapping busily. Something had gone very wrong. He wasn't sure what it was, but he knew it was bad.

He stood up and looked around. The place was almost perfectly featureless, and even though there was plenty of light he couldn't see a thing. All he could ascertain was that there was grayness on all sides.

He heard a whir of wings and a little owl settled on his shoulder, peering at him with an unfathomable expression that went well with the impenetrability of everything else.

"Could you tell me where I am?"

The owl cocked his head to one side. "Difficult to say. It's rather a sticky wicket, old boy."

"What do you mean?"

"I mean it's plain you've gotten yourself surrounded by an invisible fence."

Sir Oliver didn't believe in invisible fences. Not until he walked up and poked gingerly at its supposed surface.

His finger didn't go through it.

There seemed to be no way around it.

He mentioned this to the owl.

"Of course," said the owl. "That's because it's a side-track."

"A sidetrack? Where does it lead?"

"Sidetracks only go around in circles. It's in their nature."

"But that's not right. I can't get sidetracked now. I need to find a magic horse."

"Nothing like that here," the owl said.

"Actually, I'm looking for a golden candlestick."

"Sounds nice," said the owl, "but I don't have one."

"Even a magic ring would be nice."

The owl gave a guilty start. "Oh, the ring! I've got it right here."

The owl burrowed in his feathers, found a ring, and gave it to Oliver.

Oliver turned it in his fingers. It was a pretty ring, with a large sapphire in a plain gold setting. He thought he could see shadows move in the gem's depths.

"You shouldn't stare at that for too long," the owl said. "It's meant for doing magic, not for looking at."

"What magic? What am I supposed to do with it?"

"Haven't they told you?"

"No."

"Well, then," the owl said, "someone has been very remiss. I think you have every right to complain."

Oliver looked around, but there was no one to complain to. Only the owl.

"That's a Hell of a note," Sir Oliver said. "How am I supposed to have fine adventures if I'm stuck here?"

"We could play a hand or so of patience," the owl suggested. "To pass the time."

"I don't think so," Oliver said. "I don't play card games with birds."

The owl took a small deck of cards out from under his

wing and began to shuffle them. He gave Oliver a quizzical look.

"Go ahead, deal," Oliver said.

Soon Oliver was engrossed in the game. He had always liked patience. It helped to pass the time.

"Your deal," said the owl.

Chapter 9

Back at the inn, Azzie wiped his crystal ball and gazed into it. It remained cloudy until he remembered to say, "Show me what Sir Oliver is up to." The crystal ball flashed to acknowledge the message, and the cloudiness was replaced by a scene of Oliver in a gray foresty place, playing patience with a screech owl.

"This wasn't supposed to happen," Azzie said to himself. He needed Aretino here to lend a hand. "Where's my messenger?" the demon inquired.

The door opened and a small person walked in.

"Take this note to Aretino at once." Azzie scrawled a note with his fingernail on a parchment pad: "Come at once." He folded it twice and handed it to the messenger.

"Where will I find him?"

"In Venice, no doubt, carousing on my money."

"Could I have a spell to get there with?"

"You're supposed to have your own spells," Azzie grumbled. "But take a general one off the table there."

The messenger pocketed several from a cut-glass bowl. "To Venice!" he said to the spell, and he was off.

In his rush, Azzie had not recognized Quentin, who had taken this chance to get himself into the action.

Chapter
10

In Venice, meanwhile, Pietro Aretino had found that Azzie's cash advance had come in very handy. Aretino had always wanted to throw a really good party, one that would stand the dear old city on its ear and demonstrate yet again what a wonder Pietro Aretino was. This party had been going on for several nights and days—ever since Azzie had left.

Aretino had imported a German band for his festivities. The men had loosened their doublets and were drinking rather a lot. It was a gay and friendly time. Too bad it had to be interrupted by a messenger.

The messenger was quite young. A child, in fact, dressed in nightclothes, a handsome young boy with a full head of blond curls. It was Quentin, still slightly breathless from hanging on while the spell he had taken from Azzie whirled him over the Alps and down to Venice.

When the servant brought him to Aretino, he made a sweeping bow and said, "Aretino, I bring you a message."

"I really don't need it just now," Aretino said. "This is all turning out quite amusing."

"It's from Azzie," Quentin said. "He wants you to come at once."

"I see. And who are you?"

"I'm one of the pilgrims. You see, when my sister Puss, that's short for Priscilla, went to sleep, I decided to poke

around a little myself. I wasn't really asleep, you see. I
hardly ever am. So I went up to the second floor. I saw a
door and I peeked in, and the next thing I knew, I was in
the messenger business."

"But how are you able to get around?" Aretino asked.
"You are a mortal like me, aren't you?"

"Of course. I took a handful of spells from Azzie."

"I hope that's true," Aretino said thoughtfully. "What
does Azzie require of me?"

"Your presence, immediately."

"Where is he?"

"I'll take you to him. By magic spell," Quentin said.

"Are you quite sure those spells are trustworthy?"

Quentin didn't dignify this with an answer. He had
gotten quite accustomed to spells in a short time, and he
could hardly wait to tell Puss that traveling by domestic
spell was no big deal.

Chapter 11

Azzie had planned to celebrate when Sir Oliver was finally on his way through the passageway, for it meant that his immorality play was well begun. All Aretino had to do was observe Oliver's progress and then record it. But no sooner was the knight launched than it became obvious that he was experiencing difficulties.

Azzie lost no time looking into what had gone wrong. He traced Sir Oliver's journey into the realm of faery, utilizing those telltale signs by means of which Evil is able to follow the progress of Innocence. And so Azzie went to the strange realm in the forest in which the lands of reality and those of faery were commingled.

After a long tramp through the gloomy corridors of the forest, Azzie came to a clearing. At the end of it he saw Sir Oliver, sitting on a log, with an owl perched opposite him. They were playing cards with a small, narrow deck, one just the right size to permit the owl to hold them in his claws.

Azzie didn't know whether to laugh or cry; he had intended Sir Oliver for great deeds. Azzie hurried over, saying, "Hey, Oliver! Stop kidding around and get going!"

But his words weren't heard, and he was unable to get closer than about twenty feet from the pilgrim. Some sort of rubbery invisible wall blocked his path. The wall seemed to be soundproof as well, and perhaps was even able to block or distort vision waves, for Oliver was unable to see him.

Azzie walked around the invisible circle until he came to a point exactly opposite where Sir Oliver's gaze would have to fall if he chanced to look up. Azzie poised himself at that place and waited. After a moment, Oliver's eyes raised, and he seemed to look right through Azzie. He soon returned to his card game.

Azzie knew something uncanny was going on, something beyond the usual tomfoolery of which he was a master. He wondered who had taken a hand here.

His first suspicion was of Babriel, but this seemed to be beyond the angel's mental powers to conceive and execute. Who did that leave? Michael? It somehow didn't have Michael's finely polished touch. It was not Michael's sort of thing—but driven to desperation, Michael might be capable of anything.

That left only Ylith. He wouldn't put it past her! But what, specifically, had she done?

A moment later, she was standing beside him. "Hi, Azzie," she said. "Unless I miss my witch's guess, you were thinking about me." Her smile was simple and beautiful, and it gave away nothing.

"What have you done here?" Azzie asked.

"I thought up a bit of mischief I could do you," Ylith said. "It's standard-gauge invisible fencing."

"Very cute," Azzie said. "Now take it down!"

Ylith walked up to the invisible fence and felt around. "That's odd," she said.

"What's odd?" Azzie asked.

"I can't find the anomaly that powers the fence. It was supposed to be right here."

"This is just too much," Azzie said. "I'm going to Ananke."

Chapter 12

Ananke had invited her old friends the Three Fates over for tea. Lachesis had baked a cake for the occasion, Clotho had hunted through the souvenir shops of Babylon until she found just the right gift, and Atropos had brought a small book of poems.

Ananke generally didn't let herself appear in human form. "Just call me an old iconoclast," she was fond of saying. "I don't believe that anything really important should be capable of being pictured." But today, just to be social, and because she liked the Three Fates, she had gotten herself up as a rather large middle-aged German woman in a tailored suit and with her hair in a bun.

Ananke and the Fates were having their picnic on the slopes of Mt. Icon. Thyme and rosemary perfumed the air of the upland meadows. The sky was a deep blue, and occasional little clouds gamboled by like albino rats.

Ananke was pouring tea when Lachesis noticed a dot in the sky. It was coming toward them.

"Look!" she cried. "Someone is coming!"

"I left word I was not to be disturbed," Ananke grumbled. Who had dared disobey her? As supreme principle in the world, or at least very close to that, Ananke was accustomed to people cowering at her name. She liked to think of herself as She Who Must Be Obeyed, although that was a little grandiose.

The dot resolved itself into a figure, and the figure, in turn, could soon be seen as a flying demon.

Azzie made a graceful landing close to the picnic area. "Greetings!" he cried, bowing. "Sorry to disturb you. I hope you are all well?"

"Tell me what this is about," Ananke said sternly. "It had better be good."

"That it is," Azzie said. "I have decided to mount a new kind of play in the world, an immorality play, to act as partial counter to the many morality plays which my opponents unleashed upon the world and whose propaganda value is as insensate as it is senseless."

"You've disturbed my picnic to bring me news of your play? I know you of old, you scamp, and I am not interested in your little games. What does this play have to do with me?"

"My opponents are interfering with my production," Azzie said. "And you are preferring their side to mine."

"Well, Good's nice," Ananke said, somewhat defensively.

"Granted. But I am still allowed to oppose it, am I not? And you are here to make sure I can make my point."

"Well, that's all true," Ananke admitted.

"Then you'll stop Michael and his angels from interfering with me?"

"I suppose so. Now leave us to get on with our picnic." And with that, Azzie had to be content.

PART SEVEN

Chapter
1

Michael was in his office, relaxing in Plato's original Ideal Form of an Armchair—the archetype of all armchairs, and by definition the best ever conceived. All he lacked now was a cigar. But smoking was a vice he had given up long ago, so he really didn't lack anything.

Contentment is as hard for an archangel to find as it is for a man, so Michael was by no means taking this moment for granted. He was enjoying it to the fullest even while wondering, somewhere at the back of his mind, how long this bliss would last.

There was a knock at the door.

Michael had a sense that whatever came through was not going to please him. He considered not answering. Or saying, "Go away." But he decided against that. When you're an archangel, the buck stops at your office door.

"Come in," he said.

The door opened and a messenger entered.

The messenger was small, a child with golden curly locks, clad in nightclothes, with a package in one hand and a bunch of spells in the other. It was Quentin, who was getting on with his messenger business with a vengeance.

"Got a package for the Archangel Michael."

"That's me," Michael said.

"Sign here," Quentin said.

Michael scribbled his signature on the gold-leaf bill of lading Quentin handed him. The boy folded it and put it away, and gave the heavy package to Michael.

"You aren't an angel, are you?" Michael asked.

"No, sir."

"You're a little human boy, aren't you?"

"I believe I am," Quentin said.

"Then why are you working in a supernatural messenger service?"

"I don't really know," Quentin said. "But it's loads of fun. Is there anything else?"

"I suppose not," Michael said.

Quentin turned on his spell and was gone.

Michael scratched his head, then turned to his package. It was wrapped in plain gray paper. He tore it open and removed a large brick made of brass. Turning the brick over, he saw writing. Holding the thing up to the light so he could make out the letters, he read: "Michael! Stop interfering at once with the demon Azzie's play. Go put on your own play if you want, but stop being swinish about Azzie's. Yours faithfully, Ananke."

Michael put down the brick, his mood entirely ruined. Who did Ananke think she was, giving orders to an archangel? He had never really accepted the notion that Necessity, Ananke, ruled both Good and Bad. Who said it had to be that way? Sloppy planning, that's what it was. He wished God hadn't gone away. He was the only one who could really arbitrate this mess. But He had gone away, and somehow this Ananke person had been left in charge. And now here she was trying to tell Michael what to do.

"She can't make laws against me like that," Michael said. "Maybe she's Destiny, but she isn't God."

He decided he'd better do something about it.

A little checking by Research showed him there were several ways of doing something about Azzie's play. Simple delay might be enough.

Chapter
2

"Try again," Hephaestus said.

"I am trying!" Ganymede said. "I tell you, I can't get through."

All the gods were clustered around their side of the interface, the other side of which was Pandora's box in Westfall's chambers on Earth. This was the route Zeus had taken to free himself, and now all of the gods and goddesses wanted out, but the interface refused to allow them through. Hephaestus, the craftsman of the gods, had tried various tricks to enlarge the passage. He had never worked on interfaces before, though.

It suddenly gave off a faint humming sound, and they all stepped back. A moment later Zeus walked through and stood before them in all his strength and glory.

"So the great man returns!" Hera said. She always had had a bitter tongue in her mouth.

"Peace, woman," Zeus said.

"Easy enough for you to say," Hera said. "You get to play your dirty little games out in the world while we stay imprisoned here in this hateful place. What kind of a chief god do you think you are?"

"The very best," Zeus replied. "I have not been idle. I have a plan. But you must do what I say, for your very freedom depends on it, and upon your cooperating rather than squabbling as you usually do. I understand Michael the Archangel is coming here soon."

"Hah! The enemy!" cried Phoebus Apollo.

"No," said Zeus, "a potential ally. He is going to come here and ask for something. We must speak to him reasonably and do what he requires."

"And then?"

"And then, children, it will be our chance to take over the world again."

"Ah, it's the new fellow!" Zeus said when Michael finally arrived.

The archangel found it hateful, the way Zeus referred to him as the new fellow—as if he were some recently jumped-up deity, rather than a spiritual being of a power equal to Zeus'.

"Mind your manners," he said to Zeus. "We still have powers capable of blasting you and your half-naked crew of sybarites to the deepest Hell."

"We just came from there," Zeus said. "Once the worst has happened, it doesn't have quite the same power over you as before. Anyhow, what did you want to see me about?"

"You are aware, I suppose," said Michael, "that a new power has entered the cosmic stage?"

"The matter has not escaped our attention," said Zeus. "What about it?"

"You know of this immorality play that the demon Azzie is trying to stage?"

"I've heard about it," Zeus said. "Seems a cute idea to me."

"If it has the effect on mankind that I expect, it will serve you no better than it will us."

"How do you figure? We Greek deities don't have much truck with notions of Good and Evil."

"This scheme is beyond Good and Evil."

"Well . . . So?"

"This scheme is not only amoral, it undermines the idea that Character is Fate."

"What? What was that?" Zeus asked.

"I thought that would gain your attention," Michael said. "But that is not all. Not only is Azzie's play going to prove that Character is not even Fate, but also it will demonstrate that the Unexamined Life is Well Worth Living."

"That is too much!" Zeus said. "How can we put a stop to it?"

"We need to pursue the tactics of delay," Michael said. "There's nothing I can do personally. I have already been warned by Ananke. But if you—or, better, one of your children—would care to do a little favor for me . . ."

Phoebus arose. He smiled. "I would be delighted to help," he said. "Just tell me what it is you want me to do."

"It would involve the Cyclops," Michael said. "I would have something similar to what Phoebus set up for Odysseus. Only this time better. After that I'll have another little job for whoever among you does storms and rain and high wind."

Athena thought a while, then said, "We divided that function among many gods, including Poseidon and you yourself, great Zeus."

"That's true," Zeus said. "Well, we'll assign the weather job to someone. Ares, how would you like a really natural way of making war?"

"As long as it hurts people, it's okay with me," said Ares.

"Now listen up," Michael said. "There are a few points you need to know about weather making."

Chapter 3

A woman's voice cried, "Found it!" and there followed a click. Moments later came the sounds of a fence falling.

Oliver rose to his feet to explore the limits of his confines.

There were no limits. So he began walking.

He wasn't sure where he was going, but since he had a Moronia spell he figured it would all come out all right. The spell pulled and tugged at him, and there was no doubt as to what direction he was intended to walk. He became aware that he was covering great distances. The spell began tugging him to the left, and he followed it.

Soon he was on a beach. He continued walking, and after a while he saw a great cave. There was something forbidding about that cave, and he thought to give it a wide berth, but then he saw a rustic sign nailed up above its entrance: RINGHOLDERS WELCOME. So he went in.

A giant sat on a stool just inside the doorway. "Have you got the ring?" the giant asked.

"Sure do," Oliver said, and showed it.

The giant studied it carefully. "Good, you're the one."

The giant got up and rolled a boulder toward the entrance of the cave.

"What did you do that for?" Oliver asked.

"Orders," said the giant, sitting down again on his stool.

"So what happens now?" Oliver asked.

"Believe me, you don't want to know."

"But I do want to know. Tell me!"

"I eat you," the giant said.

"You're not serious!"

"I am perfectly serious. Did you ever know a giant to kid around?"

Oliver said, "I've never done you any harm."

"It's got nothing to do with that."

"What has it to do with, then?"

"Sorry, buddy, but I've got the work order right here. Eat the guy with the ring. That's what it says."

"What guy with what ring?" Oliver asked.

"It doesn't say. Just 'the guy with the ring.'"

"But that could be anyone."

"Look, buddy, maybe they didn't have time to spell it out any more than that."

"But what if you get the wrong guy?"

"Well, that would be somebody's tough luck, but it wouldn't be my fault if I did."

"Of course not," Oliver said. "But they'd blame you anyway."

"How do you figure?"

"Don't they blame you anyway when something goes wrong, whether it's your fault or not?"

"You got that right," the giant said. He moved back into the cave. He had an easy chair in back, and a bed and a lantern.

Oliver looked around for a weapon, but there wasn't anything he could use. He did see, though, that a piece of paper was pinned to the giant's shirt.

"What's that attached to your shoulder?" Oliver asked.

"It's the dispatch ticket they gave me."

"What does it say?"

"Just that I'm to stay here till the guy with the ring shows up."

"Does it say anything else?"

"Not that I can see."

"Let me look."

The giant didn't think this was such a good idea. He was protective of his dispatch ticket, and he wasn't about to show it to some stranger. Especially not one he was going to eat.

Oliver could understand all that, but now he was determined to get a look at the ticket. The only thing he could think of was to offer the giant a back rub.

"Why should I want a back rub?" the giant asked suspiciously.

"Because it feels good, that's why."

"I feel okay," the giant said, though it was apparent he didn't.

"Sure," Oliver said, "I can see that you feel okay. But what's okay? Okay isn't much. It's almost nothing at all. How would you like to feel good?"

"I don't know if I need this," the giant said.

"How long is it since you felt good? I mean really good?"

"I guess it's been quite a while. Nobody cares how a giant feels. Nobody even thinks a giant has feelings. No one inquires about his health or his general state of mind. People think giants are stupid, but we're smart enough to know that people don't give a damn about us."

"You got that right," Oliver said. "What about the back rub?"

"Okay," the giant said. "But do I gotta take off my shirt?"

"Not if you don't want to."

The giant lay down on the long slab of rock that he used for a bed. During the day, he made it up into a couch with boulders that resembled pillows.

Oliver pushed up the giant's shirt. He began to pound and knead the giant's back, gently at first, but then with more force as the giant complained he couldn't feel a thing. Oliver pounded and slapped and hammered, all the time trying to get a look at the ticket attached with a bronze staple to the left shoulder of the shirt.

At last he was able to make out what was written on the ticket: "This giant is vulnerable only under the left armpit, which is unarmored due to the need for ventilation. The giant should be careful not to let anything near this area." There was a manufacturer's mark under the writing, but it was blurred.

So that was something, but not really enough, because Oliver had no idea how he was going to get at the giant's left armpit. Even the right one was inaccessible.

A shadow crossed the cave door, and Oliver looked up. Standing there was a tall, well-dressed Italian-looking fellow.

"Hi, there, I'm Aretino," the man said. "Azzie sent me. If you're quite finished with your massage, do you think we could get back to work?"

"Who's that?" the giant asked sleepily.

"Don't be alarmed," Oliver said. "It's someone for me."

"Tell him to go away. After the massage I'm supposed to eat you."

Oliver rolled his eyes and took his hand from the giant's back long enough to make an imploring gesture.

Aretino now became aware of the giant. He walked slowly into the cave, keeping alert in case there were any more giants around. He whispered to Oliver, "Is he armored?"

"Yes," said Oliver. "Everywhere but his left armpit."

"You're going to have to catch him stretching."

"Sure. But how?"

Aretino whispered, "Are there any grapes around?"

"I'll ask," Oliver said, catching on at once.

"Grapes? What do you want with grapes?"

"Last meal before I die. It's the custom."

"I never heard of it. But I guess we could find you some grapes. That was a pretty good massage."

The giant heaved himself to his feet. "Come with me." He led Oliver outside. Quite near the cave was a very tall grape arbor.

"I can't reach them," said Oliver.

"Here, let me hand you down some." The giant stretched out his arm, in a movement that exposed his armpit. Aretino threw Oliver his sword; Oliver caught it. The giant's arm was still up there. But it was the right arm. Oliver hesitated.

"Go for it anyway!" Aretino called out.

Oliver gritted his teeth and plunged the sword into the giant's armpit. It was armored, just as he'd feared, but not very well armored. Aretino's sword passed into it.

"Ouch! What did you do that for?"

"I had to. You were going to kill me."

"I would have changed my mind."

"But how was I to know that?"

The giant fell to the ground. He gnashed his teeth. "I suppose I should have expected this. Whoever heard of giants winning? By the way, that candlestick you've been looking for. I've got it in the back of the cave." He gave a convulsive heave and was dead.

"Quick!" Aretino said. "Get the candlestick!"

Oliver ran back into the cave and found the candlestick behind a boulder. Now he had the ring, the key, and the candlestick. He took two steps forward and recoiled.

Aretino was gone. An entirely different man was standing in front of him.

Chapter
4

"Who are you?" Oliver asked.

"Your second-in-command, sir," the man said. "Globus is the name. Serving greatness is the game."

Oliver's peripheral vision kicked in, and he realized he was in a different place. Picking up the candlestick seemed to have done the trick. The beach was gone. He was standing in a large meadow outside a village with mountains to one side and a wide plain to the other. A river sparkled in the middle of the plain; near the edge of the river was an encampment full of men and tents.

"What troop is that?" Oliver asked.

"The White Company," Globus told him.

The White Company was famous. Its original commander, Sir John Hawkwood, had led this group to many notable victories all over Italy. There were about ten thousand of them, fighting men from every corner of Europe — swarthy Letts, pixie-haired Poles, mustached Germans, Italians with rings in their ears, Frenchmen with marcelled hair, Scotsmen with tufted eyebrows. These troops were the finest, the merriest, the bloodthirstiest, yet also the most obedient to orders, of all the troops in the civilized — even in the uncivilized — world.

"Where is Hawkwood?" Oliver asked, inquiring after the company's famous commander.

"Sir John is taking a paid leave in England," Globus

told him. "He didn't want to go, but my master paid him a price he couldn't refuse."

"Who is your master?"

"I'll not name him directly," Globus said, "except to say that he's a Hell of a good fellow. He bade me give you this."

From his haversack Globus took a long slim instrument and handed it to Oliver. Oliver recognized it at once as a baton of command, such as a field marshal might carry.

"This is your insignia of command," Globus said. "You will show this to the men and they will follow you anywhere."

"Where am I supposed to go?"

"We are situated just now on the south side of the Alps." Globus pointed in a southerly direction. "It's a straight march down that way and along the river to Venice."

"All I have to do is lead the men there?" Oliver asked.

"That's it."

"Then let us go join the men!" Oliver cried exultantly.

Chapter
5

Oliver reached the purple tent that had been reserved for him. Inside, sitting on a campstool and filing his nails with a little silver file, was none other than Azzie.

"Hi, Chief!" Oliver cried.

"Welcome to your command, Field-Marshal," Azzie said. "Is everything to your liking?"

"It's wonderful," Oliver said. "You've gotten me a wonderful bunch of soldiers. I had a look at some of them as I came up here. Real toughs, aren't they? Anybody trying to stand against me is going to be very sorry. Is there anyone I have to fight, by the way?"

"Of course. On your march south, which I expect you to begin immediately after we finish this briefing, you will encounter the Berserkers of the Death's Head Brigade."

"They sound tough. Do you really think I should start out fighting guys who are tough?"

"They're not tough at all. I gave them that name because it sounds good to the press. Actually they're a bunch of disenfranchised local peasants, farmers from the district who have been put off their land for nonpayment of the exorbitant taxes. They are armed only with axes and scythes, have no armor, no bows and arrows, not even proper lances. Also there are only a couple of hundred of them against your ten thousand. Not only are these men poorly prepared, they are also guaranteed to betray their comrades and flee at the first clash of arms."

"That sounds okay," Oliver said. "And then what?"

"Then you'll march into Venice. We'll have the press prepared."

"The press? Surely I haven't done anything to warrant torture!"

"You don't understand," Azzie said. " 'Press' is our name for the various persons who make things known to other people: painters, poets, scriveners, that sort of thing."

"I don't know anything about that," Oliver said.

"You'd better learn if you expect to become famous for your victories. How will you become legendary unless the writers write about you?"

"I guess I thought it just happened," Oliver said.

"Not at all. I've hired the finest poets and writers of the age, headed by the Divine Aretino, to sing your praises. Titian will do a huge propaganda poster of whatever victory we ask him to portray. And I'll hire a composer to write a masque in memory of the victory, whatever it is going to be."

Azzie rose and walked to the entrance of the tent. A few fat drops of rain were falling, and big black clouds had come up from behind the Alps. "Looks like a bit of weather making up," he said. "It'll blow over soon, no doubt, and you can get your men on the road to Venice. Don't worry about how to address them, or in what language. Just tell Globus and he'll make sure everyone understands."

"Good. I was worried about that," said Oliver, who hadn't thought about it at all but wanted to sound alert.

"Good luck," Azzie said. "I suppose I'll see you in Venice by and by."

PART EIGHT

Chapter
1

Darkness held sway over Europe, and nowhere more than in the little inn where Azzie—despite small journeys of reconnaissance and aid—was still busily recruiting people for his play.

"What news, Aretino?" Azzie asked.

"Why, sir, Venice already buzzes with rumors that something strange and unprecedented is going on. No one knows what, but there is talk. Venetians are not privy to the secrets of the Supernaturals, though we certainly ought to be, so special are we among the peoples of the world. Citizens meet day and night in San Marco's Square to discuss the latest marvel glimpsed in the sky. But you did not send for me, sir, to discuss gossip."

"I've called you here, my dear Pietro, so that you might meet some of my contestants at firsthand, the better to assist them as they go about their work for me. It's a pity you missed Sir Oliver. He's a right fine model of a knight, and I think he'll do us proud."

"I caught a glimpse of him as I was riding up," Aretino said without much enthusiasm. "It's a rather unusual way to cast a play, taking the first applicant and giving him the role willy-nilly. But no doubt he'll do. Who's next?"

"We wait and see," Azzie said. "If I am not mistaken, those are footfalls upon the stairs."

"They are indeed," Aretino said, "and by their sound I

judge them to belong to a person of no particular quality in terms of station in life."

"How can you say so? I'd love to know your secret of distant perceptions."

Aretino smiled sagely. "You'll note that the boots make a scraping sound, even when heard through the material of a door and from the distance of half a corridor. That, sir, is the unmistakable sound of untanned leather. Since the sound is high-pitched, one must ascertain that the boots are stiff, and that the one rubbing against the other is like two pieces of metal rubbing together. No man of quality would wear such material, so it must belong to a poor man."

"Five ducats if you're right," Azzie said. The sound of the boots stopped just outside the door. There was a knock. "Come in," said the redheaded demon.

The door opened and a man entered slowly, looking both ways as if unsure of his reception. He was a tall yellow-headed fellow wearing a ragged shirt of homespun and boots of cowhide that looked as if they had been annealed to his legs.

"I'll pay you later," Azzie said to Aretino. To the stranger he said, "I do not know you, sir. Are you part of our pilgrimage, or did you come upon us in the dark?"

"In a corporeal sense, I'm one of the group," the stranger replied, "yet in a spiritual sense I am not one of the party."

"The fellow hath a pretty wit," Azzie said. "What is your name, fellow, and your station in life?"

"They call me Morton Kornglow," the man said. "My regular occupation is grooming horses, but I was impressed into the job of valet to Sir Oliver, since I live in his ancestral village and have always been handy with a currycomb. Thus I may fairly claim that I am one of you as far as the physical body is concerned, but a company is generally thought of as composed of like-minded members, and one does not include the dogs and cats who may stray along with them, nor the servants, who are no more than the animals, though perhaps a little more valuable. I must ask you at once, sir, does my lowly station in life bar me from participating in this event? Is your contest open only to nobles, or may a common man with dirt under his fingernails volunteer?"

"In the Spiritual World," Azzie said, "the distinctions men make between each other are meaningless. We think of you all as souls for the taking, wearing a temporary body and soon to give it up. But enough of that. Would you be one of our seekers of the candlesticks, Kornglow?"

"I would indeed, sir demon," Kornglow said. "For though I am but a commoner, there is that which I desire. I would go to a bit of trouble to procure it."

"Name your desire," Azzie said.

"Before you joined our company we took a side trip to visit the estates of Rodrigo Sforza. The gentles ate at high table, whereas common folk like myself sat in the kitchen. Through its open door we could view all of the proceedings, and there it was that I laid eyes upon Cressilda Sforza, wife of Lord Sforza himself. Sir, she is the loveliest of women, with hair of cornsilk yellow lying smooth upon a cheek of damask blush that would put shame to the angels. She hath a tiny waist, sir, and above it doth swell—"

"That'll be enough," Azzie said. "Spare us the rest of your rustic pleasantries and tell me what you want of the lady."

"Why, that she should marry me, of course," Kornglow said.

Aretino gave a great laugh and muffled it forthwith as

a cough. Even Azzie had to smile, so ill-matched was the loutish and out-at-elbow Kornglow with any pretty noble-woman.

"Well, sir," Azzie said, "you are not afraid to shoot high in your courting!"

"A poor man can aspire to Helen of Troy if he so desires," said Kornglow. "And in his fancy she may well respond to him above all men, and find him more desirable than delectable Paris himself. In a dream, whatever you want can happen. And is this not a sort of a dream, Your Excellency?"

"Yes, I suppose it is," Azzie said. "Well, sir, if we were to grant your wish, we'd have to have you ennobled in order that there be no impediment of station to the marriage ceremony."

"I'd be willing," Kornglow said.

"We'd also have to get Lady Cressilda's consent," Aretino pointed out.

"Leave that to me when the time comes," Azzie said. "Well, it's a challenge, Kornglow, but I think we can swing it."

Aretino frowned and said, "There's the fact that the lady is already married, my lord, that might stand as some impediment."

"We have clerks in Rome to take care of details like that," Azzie said. He turned to Kornglow. "There are a few things you will have to do. Are you ready to go to a little trouble?"

"Why, yes, sir, so long as it be not too strenuous. A man should not be taken out of his native temper even by the most outrageous of good fortune, and my own native temper is of a laziness so extreme that did the world but know about it they'd declare me a prodigy."

"There's nothing too difficult ahead of you," Azzie

promised. "I think we can dispense with the usual sword fighting, since you were not educated to it."

Azzie fished in his waistcoat pocket and found one of his magical keys. He handed it to Kornglow, who turned it over and over in his fingers.

"You will go from here," Azzie said, "and the key will take you to a doorway. You will pass through it, and find a magic horse with a magic candlestick in his saddlebag. Mounting him, you will find your adventure, and, at the end of it, your Cressilda of the cornsilk hair."

"Great!" Kornglow said. "It is wonderful when good fortune comes easy like this!"

"Yes," Azzie said, "ease of acquisition is one of the great things of this world, and a moral I hope to preach to men: namely, good fortune comes easy, so why sweat it?"

"It is a wonderful moral!" Kornglow said. "I love this story!" Clutching the key, he rushed out of the room.

Azzie smiled benignly. "Another happy customer."

"There's someone new at the door," said Aretino.

Chapter 2

Mother Joanna sat in her room at the inn. She was more than a little afraid.

Outside, in the hallways, she could hear occasional scuffling sounds. They might have come from anything, natural or supernatural, but Joanna suspected they emanated from pilgrims who had decided to take Sir Antonio up on his offer and were on their way to his chambers.

Despite her holy office, Joanna was not unacquainted with human desire. There were things she wanted for herself, and, not being a moderate person, these desires burned in her immoderately. She was a political mother superior, not a religious one, and had looked upon her job much as the taking on of any other great enterprise. Her nunnery at Gravelines, with its seventy-two nuns and a host of servants and people to look after the animals, was an enterprise similar to that of a small town. Joanna had reveled in it from the very beginning. She might have been made for this. She had never been like other little girls, playing with dolls and dreaming of marriage. Even as a child she had been fond of giving orders to her birds and spaniels—You sit there, and you there—scolding them while she gave them tea.

This practice of giving orders had not left her when she grew to womanhood. Matters might have been different had she been beautiful, but she had taken after the Mortimer side of the family. She had the great white face of the

Mortimers, the short, dry, lifeless hair, the stocky body more suited to laboring with spade and plough than to the languors of the pursuits of love. She wanted to be rich, and feared by all, and service in the Church had seemed the way to get it. She was conventionally pious, but her piety ran afoul of her practicality, which told her that here was an opportunity to get what she wanted rather than waiting forever until the Pope was induced to advance her to some larger nunnery.

She thought and thought, and she paced up and down her little room, taking note of her desires and asking herself which of them was paramount. Each time she heard a sound outside, she started; it seemed that all of the others were taking advantage of Sir Antonio's offer to give them their hearts' desires. Soon the required seven would be made up, and she would have no further chance. Finally she decided to act.

Mother Joanna crept out of her chamber and made her way silently down the inn's dark passageways. She climbed the stairs to the second level and winced when they creaked. Coming at last to the door to Sir Antonio's room, she took her courage into her hands, reached up, and tapped lightly upon it.

Azzie's voice from the other side said, "Come in, my dear. I've been expecting you."

She had many questions. Azzie found her tiresome, but he managed to reassure her. When he came to inquire as to her heart's desire, however, he found her less than forthcoming. A look of sad embarrassment came across her broad white face.

"What I want," she said, "is something I do not even care to speak about. It is too shameful, too demeaning."

"Come on," Azzie said. "If you can't tell your demon, who can you tell?"

Joanna seemed about to speak, then, jerking a thumb at Aretino, said, "What about him? Must he hear, too?"

"Of course. He is our poet," Azzie said. "How else can he record our adventures save he be present? To make no record of these notable adventures were crime indeed, one that would condemn us to the vast unconsciousness of unrecorded life in which most people live out their lives. But Aretino will immortalize us, my dear! Our poet will take our exploits, no matter how slight they might seem, and weave them into deathless verse."

"Well, sir demon, you persuade me," Joanna said. "I confess to you, then, that ever in my dreams I would be a great righter of wrong of the public sort, receiving all manner of adulation in ballads for my accomplishments. Something like a female Robin Hood—with lots of time in between exploits for hunting."

"I'll figure out something," Azzie said. "We'll get started right away. Take this key." He told Mother Joanna what was coming up in the way of rings, doorways, magic candlesticks, and magic horses, and sent her on her way.

"And now, Aretino," Azzie said, "I think we have time for a tankard of wine before the next supplicant. How do you think it's going so far?"

"Frankly, sir, I have no idea. Plays are usually laid out beforehand, with everything made clear in advance. In this drama of yours, all is muddy and uncertain. What does this fellow Kornglow stand for? Is he Overweening Pride? Bucolic Humor? Unquenchable Courage? And Mother Joanna—is she to be despised or pitied? Or a little of both?"

"It is confusing, isn't it?" Azzie said. "But very lifelike, I think you'll agree."

"Oh, no doubt. But how are we to find suitable moral dicta in all this?"

"Don't worry, Aretino, no matter what the characters do, we'll find a way of making it represent what we have been speaking about all along. The playwright gets the last word, you must remember, and therefore is in a position to say that his idea is proven whether it is or not. Now pass that bottle this way."

Chapter
3

When Kornglow returned to the corner of the old stable he was more than a little surprised to see a horse tethered where there had been none before. It was a tall white stallion, and its ears pricked forward as Kornglow approached it. How had this noble steed gotten here? Then he saw that he was in a different place entirely from where he'd thought he was. The magic key must have led him through one of those doorways Azzie had been speaking about, and his adventure could already be launched.

He had to make sure. Espying the saddlebags that the horse wore, Kornglow opened the one nearest him and reached in. His hand encountered something massy and metallic, thin, and long. He pulled it halfway out. A candlestick! And unless he missed his guess, it was made of solid gold. He slid it back carefully into the saddlebag.

The horse whinnied at him, as though inviting him to get up and ride away, but Kornglow shook his head, left the stable, and looked around outside. The stately manor house not twenty yards from him was unmistakably the house of Lord Rodrigo Sforza, the selfsame house where Kornglow had had his first and only glimpse of Lady Cressilda.

It was her house. She was inside.

But Lord Sforza was also undoubtedly inside. As were his servants, retainers, guards, torturers . . .

There was no sense in rushing into this. Compunction

cast its dark wings over him, and Kornglow took thought. Now, for the first time, he considered his adventure, and found it more than a little daft. It was always nobles who were doing this sort of thing. Well, sometimes commoners were involved in the folktales. But was he the stuff folk-story heroes were made of? He doubted it. He knew he was gifted with a swift turn of fantasy; otherwise he wouldn't have gotten himself into this in the first place. But was he the man to persevere through it? Was the lady worth it?

"Why, sir," said a soft voice at his elbow, "you do bend your gaze on the manor house as if someone very special were awaiting you there."

Kornglow turned. Beside him was a diminutive milk-maid in peekaboo bodice and full pleated skirt. She had tousled dark curly hair, a pert expression, a full and curvaceous figure for so small a person, and a smile that was both gentle and lascivious. An unbeatable combination.

"That's Lord Sforza's house, isn't it?" Kornglow asked.

"That it is," the milkmaid said. "Were you thinking of kidnapping Lady Cressilda?"

"Why do you say that?" Kornglow asked.

"Because it cuts directly to the heart of the matter," the woman said. "There's a game afoot, put forth by a certain demon who is known to friends of mine."

"He said Lady Cressilda would be mine," Kornglow said.

"Easy enough for him to promise," the woman said. "I am Leonore, a simple milkmaid to all appearances, but in truth rather more, I assure you. I am here to tell you that the lady you're considering tying yourself to is a bitch of purest nastiness supreme. Winning her will be like damning yourself to the deepest pit of Hell."

Kornglow was much surprised at this speech. He looked at Leonore with an interest that grew more intense as the seconds passed by. "Lady," he said, "I know not what to do. Could you perchance advise me?"

"That I could," Leonore said. "I will read your palm, and that will tell all. Come over here where we can be comfortable."

She led him back into the stable, to a corner where the hay was piled in soft comfortable heaps. Her eyes were wide and wild and had the color of magic, and her touch was featherlight. Taking his hand, she drew him down beside her.

Chapter
4

All reports seemed to show that Azzie's projected play was exciting considerable attention across the Spiritual World, that there was even betting going on, and that upsets seemed to be happening. The main upset of course was the sudden release of the old gods. Zeus and that lot. These were many matters that needed Michael's urgent attention, and it was with this in mind that he agreed to see the angel Babriel.

Babriel's interview with the archangel took place in the executive boardroom of the Heaven Gate Office Building in downtown Central Heaven. Heaven Gate was a lofty and inspiring building, and the angels loved to work there. Next to the ineffable joy they felt at being close to the Highest, there was also the pleasure of working inside an architectural gem.

It was early evening, and a gentle rain was falling over the City of Good Vibes, as Central Heaven was also called. Babriel hurried down the marble corridors, making little twenty- and thirty-foot soaring flights to save time even though there were signs everywhere saying NO FLYING IN THE CORRIDORS.

He came at last to Michael's suite of offices in the right wing, knocked, and entered.

Michael was at his desk, with various reference works open on the table around him. A computer hummed softly to one side. The lighting was soft and golden.

"About time," Michael said, with a momentary show of pique. "I've got to send you out again at once."

"What's up, sir?" Babriel asked, sitting in one of the upholstered love seats facing the archangel's desk.

"This situation with Azzie and his play is even more serious than we'd anticipated. It seems our demon has acquired a variance from Ananke herself, giving him express permission to perform miracles in the furtherance of his plan. Furthermore, Ananke has ruled that we of the Light are not to be accorded any more special privileges simply because we are Good. I also have it on authority that Azzie has some scheme that would abstract Venice from real time and set it up as a special entity. Do you know what that means?"

"Not exactly, sir, no, I don't."

"It means that this noisome demon can, potentially at least, rewrite history to his heart's content."

"But sir, an abstracted Venice would have no effect upon the mainstream of human history."

"That's true. But it could be used as a model for those dissatisfied souls who think history ought to be something other than what it is—an account of human tribulation and suffering. The concept of Rewriteability undermines the entire doctrine of Predestination. It releases mankind into a realm where Chance can play an even greater part than it already does."

"Hmm, that's serious, sir," Babriel said.

Michael nodded. "The very order of the cosmos could be at risk here. Our long-established preeminence is being challenged. The principle of Good itself has become moot."

Babriel gaped at him.

"But at least it does one thing for us," Michael went on.

"What's that, sir?"

"It releases us from the galling strictures of fairness. It means we can take off the gloves. This is no longer a gentleman's game. At last we can lay aside our compunctions and get in there and fight."

"Yes, sir!" Babriel said, though he hadn't been aware that too much in the way of compunctions had guided Michael's actions to date. "What, specifically, do you want me to do?"

"We have learned," Michael said, "that Azzie is onto a scheme now involving a magic horse."

Babriel nodded. "That sounds very like him."

"There's no reason we should just let that go on as he has planned. Get you to Earth, Babriel, to Lord Rodrigo Sforza's mansion, and do something about the magic horse that even now waits in the stables for Kornglow."

"To hear is to obey!" cried Babriel, springing to his feet. He flew through the corridors with a great beating of wings. This was serious!

In not much more than a trice he was back on Earth. Taking but a moment to orient himself, he flapped his way to the manor house of the Sforzas and came down lightly in the courtyard.

It was just past dawn, and the count's household was still asleep. Babriel looked around, then went to the stable. From within he heard the unmistakable sounds of a man with a maid, complete, as it was, with giggles and soft squishy noises. He heard a neighing sound, then found, tethered close by, a white stallion with finely wrought saddlebags. He soothed the noble steed and untied its reins. "Come with me, my beauty," he said.

Chapter
5

Kornglow found himself lying on a pallet of straw, caught up in a tangle of arms and legs, only half of which were his. The sun was shining brightly through cracks in the half-finished walls of the stable, and a smell of straw, dung, and horses assailed his nostrils. He untangled himself from the woman with whom he had coupled in such abandon, hastily pulled on his clothes, and got to his feet.

"Why such a rush?" Leonore asked, awakening. "Stay."

"No time, no time," Kornglow said, stuffing his shirt into his breeches and his feet into his boots. "I'm supposed to be on an adventure!"

"Forget the adventure," Leonore said. "You and I have found each other. Why ask for more?"

"No, I must not tarry! I must get on with it! Where is my magic horse?"

Kornglow searched through the stable, but the horse was nowhere to be found. All he could locate was a small piebald donkey tied to a half paling. It brayed at him, its mouth open and its yellow teeth bared. Kornglow looked at it searchingly and said, "Has some enchantment so altered my steed? It must be! If I ride it away, no doubt it will change back in the due course of time!"

He untied the donkey and mounted; he kicked it hard in the ribs, making the creature amble into the courtyard.

The animal didn't like the idea, but Kornglow urged it on. The donkey ambled across the chicken yard, past the kitchen garden, and all the way to the manor gate.

"Hello, there!" Kornglow shouted at the gate.

A man's heavy voice from within called out, "Who is out there?"

"One who would seek the hand of the Lady Cressilda!"

A large balding man in shirt and pants and chef's toque came out. Scowling and unfriendly, he said, "Have you taken leave of your senses? The lady is married! Her husband cometh even now!"

The door opened further. Out stepped a tall nobleman in fine attire, stern faced and haughty, with a rapier at his hip. "I am Rodrigo Sforza," he said in a voice that would have to be described as ominous. "What seems to be the trouble?"

The cook bowed low and said, "This lout says he comes for the hand of Cressilda, your lady wife."

Sforza fixed Kornglow with a steely gaze. "Say you so, fellow?"

Kornglow now perceived that something was wrong. His way was supposed to have been prepared for him. It was probably the loss of the magic horse that had put him in this strait.

He turned and tried to prod the donkey to a gallop. It set its heels and bucked, throwing Kornglow violently to the ground.

"Call my guards!" cried Sforza.

His men came hurrying around the corner, buckling up their doublets and strapping on their swords.

"To the dungeons with him!" cried Sforza.

And so Kornglow soon found himself in a dark hole, his head ringing from numerous blows.

Chapter
6

"Well, Morton," Azzie said, "this is a fine mess you've gotten yourself into."

Kornglow sat up, blinking. One moment before he had been alone in Sforza's dungeon, nursing his bruised head and contemplating his unhappiness. The cell had been bare, with no more than a scattering of moldy straw on its earthen floor, and there had been little Kornglow could do to make himself comfortable. But now he was outside again. Kornglow was getting awfully tired of all these sudden moves, and the strange wavelike motions they involved tended to upset his stomach.

Azzie was standing before him, splendid in a blood red cloak and soft leather boots.

"Your Excellency!" Kornglow cried. "I'm so glad to see you!"

"Are you, indeed? I'm afraid I must tell you, you have compromised your adventure before it even got properly started. How on Earth did you misplace the magic horse?"

Kornglow fell back on the excuse that all men used in that day and age. "I was tempted by a sorceress, most noble one! I am a mere man! What could I do?"

He then described his adventure with the fair Leonore. Azzie detected a familiar hand in this.

"The horse was there at the beginning of your adventure?" Azzie asked.

"Indeed it was, Your Excellency! But when I looked again, it was gone, and there was only a donkey. Could you bring me another, sir, that I might try again?"

"Magic horses aren't so easily procured," Azzie said. "If you'd known how we had to search for that one, you would have taken better care of it."

"But surely there's some other magical object we could use instead," Kornglow said. "Must it be a horse?"

"I suppose we might come up with something."

"I'll do it right this time, Your Excellency! Oh, but there is one other thing."

"What is it?" Azzie said.

"I'd like to change my wish."

Azzie stared at him. "What are you talking about?"

"I had asked for the hand of the fair Cressilda in marriage, but I've since reconsidered. She's apt to hold it against me because I'm not gently bred. But fair Leonore suits me to a T. I'd like her as my prize."

"Don't be silly," Azzie said. "We already have you down in the books as getting Cressilda."

"But she's already married!"

"You knew that beforehand. And what difference does it make?"

"Quite a lot, sir. I would still have to live in the same world as her husband. You couldn't spend all your time protecting me, could you?"

"You do have a point," Azzie said. "But you have already made your choice. Cressilda it will have to be."

"There was nothing in the agreement," Kornglow said, "that said I couldn't change my mind. Light-mindedness is one of my most salient characteristics, my lord, and it isn't fair to ask me to change my changeability."

"I'll look into it," Azzie said. "I'll let you know my decision soon."

With that he vanished, and Kornglow settled down for a nap, since there seemed nothing else to do.

But he was rudely awakened yet again; Azzie had arrived with a new white horse that anyone could tell had to be magical, so beautiful was it.

An interview with Leonore had confirmed what Azzie had suspected all along: she was not a woman of Earth at all, but rather a large elf disguising herself as a human being.

"Elves are mean-spirited," she told Azzie. "Since I am taller than most of them, they laugh at me for being a giantess, and none will marry me. As a human woman I am considered petite, and I am much beloved. If I marry a human, it is certain I will greatly outlive my husband. But I'll show him a good time while he's on Earth."

Just then, Kornglow rode up on the magic horse.

The elf-girl was suddenly shy. And who would not be when the powers of Evil had suddenly intervened to ensure one's happiness?

"My lord," Leonore said to Azzie, "I know our happiness was not your intention or concern, but I thank you for it anyhow. What do you require of my man?"

"Simply that he take you and get promptly to Venice," Azzie said. "I have a great deal for you to do once you're there, and I don't know if I'll have time to devise any adventures for you along the way."

"We will go directly, as you wish," Leonore said. "I will get Kornglow to stick to business."

And so the lovers departed, both mounted on the magic horse, on the high road toward Venice.

Azzie shook his head as he watched them go. Things weren't working out at all as he had expected. None of the actors seemed to be doing what they were supposed to. It's what came, he supposed, of not having their lines written out for them.

Chapter
7

Lady Cressilda sat in her carved rosewood chair in the deep bay window of her second-floor sitting room, a needlepoint tapestry on her lap. She was pricking out the Judgment of Paris in rose and lavender, but her mind was elsewhere. Presently she put down her work and sighed and looked out the open window. Her ash-blond hair was pulled straight back and framed her face like a dove's wing. Her small features were pensive.

It was early in the morning, but it felt already as if it would be another hot day. Below, in the courtyard, a couple of chickens were scratching at a corncob; Cressilda could also hear singing from the shed to the left where the women were doing the month's washing. The distant neighing of a horse came to her ears, and she thought she might go hunting a little later. She thought it without much enthusiasm, though, for the larger game animals, the boars and stags, had been hunted out of the surrounding woods by the generations of Sforzas who had owned this property since time out of mind. She herself was a skilled huntress; a veritable Diana, the court poets called her. But she was not interested in their silliness, any more than in Rodrigo's forced pleasantries when they met at the breakfast table from time to time.

Something white moved in the courtyard below, and Cressilda looked to see what it was. A white stallion was picking its way slowly across the hard-packed earth. It moved alertly, its proud head held high, nostrils flared. For a moment it seemed as if the shimmering outline of a winged man moved at its head, leading it. She stared at it, perplexed. She could remember no such horse in the Sforza stables, and she knew every one of them, from the newborn colts to the old warhorses put out to pasture. She also knew most of the better horses in the area, and this steed was none of them.

There was no sign of a rider about. Where could this steed have come from, with its glowing white mane and its uncanny eye? This horse was magic. . . .

She ran to the stairs, hurrying down them, through the big dusty receiving rooms, and out into the courtyard. The white horse had come up to the door. It seemed to recognize her and nodded its noble head as she approached. Cressilda stroked its velvety nose; the stallion whinnied and nodded its head.

"What are you trying to tell me?" Cressilda asked. She opened the saddlebag closest to her, hoping to find a clue to the animal's ownership. Within she found a tall candlestick that to all appearances was made of purest red gold. A note was inside, written on parchment and rolled into a screw. She straightened it out, and read, "Follow me, and wish for what you will. It will be granted."

Her wish! It had been many years since she had even thought of it. Could this noble steed be the means of accomplishing that dream? Had it been sent by Heaven itself? Or was it perchance a gift from Hell?

She cared not. She vaulted into the saddle. The stallion shivered, laid back its ears, then calmed to her touch.

"Take me to whoever sent you," Cressilda said. "I would get to the bottom of this, no matter where it takes me."

The horse broke into a smart trot.

Chapter 8

"A warhorse? You say my lady departed on a warhorse?" Lord Sforza was said to be a little slow on the uptake, but he understood horses—and he understood people riding away on them, especially his wife.

The Court thaumaturge went through it all again. "Yes, my lord. It was a horse such as no one has seen before in these parts. Pure white it was, noble of aspect, fiery of manner. My Lady Cressilda saw it, and without a moment's hesitation she vaulted to the saddle. We know not where she has gone."

"You saw all this yourself?"

"With my very own eyes, lord."

"Do you think it was a magic horse?"

"I do not know," the thaumaturge said. "But I can find out."

The interview was taking place in his alchemist's studio in the high tower. The thaumaturge lost no time stoking up the fire under his alembic; when it was roaring he poured in various powders, and the fire flared up green and then purple. He watched carefully as variously colored smokes arose. Then he turned to Sforza.

"My spirit familiars signal me that it was indeed a magic horse. We have probably seen the last of our Lady Cressilda, for ladies who ride away on magic horses rarely return, and if they do, to be frank, sir, there's no living with them."

"Damnation!" Sforza said.

"You can lodge a complaint through my familiars, sir. There may still be a chance of getting her back."

"I don't want her back," Sforza said. "I'm more than happy to be rid of her. She's no fun anymore. I'm glad Cressilda is gone. What annoys me is that she got the magic horse. They don't come around very often, do they?"

"Very seldom," he admitted.

"And she had to grab it. Maybe this horse was meant for me. How dare she take the only magic horse that's been seen in these parts since time immemorial?"

The thaumaturge spoke soft words, but Sforza would not be consoled. He stamped out of the tower and down to the manor house. He was a scholar, in his own view anyhow, and it galled him that a matter as interesting as this had come and gone before he'd had a chance even to see it. What irked him most, though, was that magic horses usually carry with them the fulfillment of a wish, and he had missed that, too. It was a chance that would never come again.

Believing so, he was utterly flabbergasted when, an hour later, he went down to his stables to loiter, he saw there was another white horse there, one he had never seen before.

It was a stallion, and it was white. Though not quite as imposing as he thought a magic horse ought to be, it looked enough like a magic horse for him. Without another thought, he swung into the saddle.

"Now we'll see!" he cried. "Take me to wherever you take people under these circumstances!"

The horse broke into a trot, then into a canter, and then a full gallop. Now we're in for it, Lord Sforza thought, hard-pressed just to hang on.

Chapter 9

It was early morning. The remaining pilgrims were in the inn, getting ready to eat their morning porridge and whole-wheat bread while their servants were getting the horses ready for the day.

Azzie was brooding up in his room, Aretino with him. The turnout of volunteers for the play had been rather disappointing.

"Why are the others holding back?" Azzie wondered aloud.

"Maybe they're frightened," Aretino suggested. "Do we really need a full seven?"

"I suppose not," Azzie said. "We'll use what we get. Maybe we should stop here."

Just then there was a knocking at the door.

"Aha!" Azzie said. "I knew we were going to get more participants. Answer the door, my dear Pietro, and we'll see who has come to us."

Aretino arose somewhat wearily, crossed the room, and opened the door. In walked a beautiful young woman, blond, with a pale complexion and grave, finely shaped lips. She wore a sky blue gown, ribbons of gold in her hair.

"Madam," Pietro said, "is there something we can do for you?"

"I think there is," the woman replied. "Are you the ones who sent the magic horse?"

"I think you want to speak with my friend here, Antonio," Pietro said.

After he had found a seat for her, Azzie admitted that yes, he had had something to do with magic horses, and yes, fulfillment of a wish did go along with each horse—and that acting in his play was the only condition for these gifts. He explained further that he was a fiend, but not a fearsome one. Quite a nice fiend, he had been told. Since this didn't seem to put Cressilda off, he asked her how she had acquired the magic horse.

"It just walked out of my stable and into my courtyard," Cressilda said. "I mounted and gave it its head. It brought me here."

"But I didn't send him to you," Azzie pointed out. "This horse was intended for someone else. Are you sure you didn't steal him, my dear?"

Cressilda drew herself up indignantly. "Dare you accuse me of horse theft?"

"No, of course not," Azzie said. "You're not the type, is she, Pietro? It must have been our friend Michael, having his little joke. Well, Cressilda, this horse does indeed introduce its owner to a world in which his or her dearest wish can come true. I happen to be short one or two players, so if you'd like to volunteer—seeing as how you have the horse already—"

"Yes!" Cressilda said. "Indeed!"

"What is your wish?" Azzie asked, expecting to hear the usual gushy nonsense about a fine young prince and a long lifetime of married bliss.

"I want to be a warrior," she said. "I know it's unusual for a woman, but we do have the example of Joan of Arc, and Boadicea before her. I want to lead men into battle."

Azzie thought about it, turning it over this way and that in his mind. It was not in his original plan, nor did

Aretino seem too eager about it. But Azzie knew he had to get his play moving, and he had already accepted the premise that he'd take more or less anyone who came along.

"I think we can do something for you," Azzie said. "I'll just need a little time to set it up."

"That will be fine," Cressilda said. "If you should see my husband, Rodrigo Sforza, by the way, you don't necessarily have to mention that I'm here."

"I am the soul of discretion," Azzie said.

When the lady had departed, Azzie sat down with Aretino to plot out a sequence. Before he could even begin, though, there was a darkening shape at the window and an insistent tapping at the pane.

"Aretino, get it, will you, there's a good fellow," Azzie said.

Aretino walked over and raised the window. In flew a small, long-tailed sprite, one of the imp family used by the Powers of Dark to carry communications back and forth. It fluttered inside when Aretino opened the window.

"You're Azzie Elbub?" the imp said. "I don't want to make any mistakes here."

"That's who I am," Azzie said. "What message have you brought me?"

"It concerns Mother Joanna," the sprite said. "And I'd better pick it up from the beginning."

Chapter 10

Mother Joanna had been riding along the high road toward Venice. She had taken a shortcut through the forest, planning to rendezvous with Sir Oliver and then proceed in his company. She was in good spirits, it being a fine day, and all the woods alive with birdsong. A soft Italian sky hung overhead, and little brooks sparkled and invited leaping over. Mother Joanna did not permit herself any such nonsense, however. She guided her magic horse at a sober pace and went on, deeper and deeper into the forest. She had just come to the darkest and gloomiest part of it when she heard an owl hoot. Mother Joanna had a sudden presentiment of danger.

"Who is there?" she cried, for the woods ahead of her suddenly seemed filled with menace.

"Stop where you are," a gruff male voice said, "or I'll put a crossbow bolt through you."

Joanna looked around wildly, but there seemed no place she could retreat to; the woods were so dense here that she couldn't even get her horse up to a decent canter. Deciding on discretion, she reined up and said, "I am a mother superior and you risk damnation if you so much as touch me."

"Glad to meet you," the gruff voice said. "I am Hugh Dancy, and I am known as the Bandit of Forest Perilous."

The branches parted, and a man stepped forward. He

was a strongly built fellow in the prime of life, black haired, wearing a leather jerkin and knee boots. Other men also came out of the tangled underbrush, about a dozen of them. From the leering expressions on their faces, Joanna could tell that they had not seen a woman in a long while.

"Get down off that horse," Hugh ordered. "You're coming back to the camp with me."

"I shall do no such thing," said Mother Joanna, and she flicked the reins. Her magic horse took two slow ambling steps forward, then stopped when Hugh seized it by the bridle.

"Get down," Hugh repeated, "or I'll pull you down."

"What do you intend?"

"To make an honest woman out of you," Hugh said. "We hold not with your churchly celibacy. We'll have you married by the end of the day to one of us."

Joanna dismounted. "Over my dead body," she said quietly.

"It matters not how," Hugh said, just as a loud crashing sound emanated from the brush.

The men blanched, casting frightened glances in all directions. The sounds grew louder as something seemed to draw nearer. "Ah! We're done for!" one of them cried. "'Tis the great wild boar!" shouted another. "Doomed," said a third.

Mother Joanna leaped from her saddle to the ground. It was not only with hawks that she had hunted.

Snatching a spear from one of the bandits, she faced herself in the direction of the crashing sounds.

Moments later, an enormous black boar burst from the brush into the clearing. She positioned herself before it, ramming the butt of the spear deep into the earth.

"Come on, you stupid pig!" she called. "We dine on pork chops tonight!"

It rushed toward her and she leaned heavily upon the spear. It impaled itself and lay flowing blood amid snuffles, twitches, and grunts. After a time, it grunted its last grunt and expired.

Placing her foot upon the carcass, she wrenched the spear free and turned toward Hugh.

"We were talking of dead bodies," she said.

He drew back, as did the others.

"We were thinking of such a delightful pastime as this," he said. "We do hope you will join us for dinner shortly."

"Aye!" cried the men as they set to butchering the boar.

"Perhaps I shall," she said.

"Thou art a veritable Diana," Hugh said, "and thou shalt be treated as such."

Chapter
11

Azzie was annoyed at the news. He was just about to ride off to rescue Mother Joanna when there was another sound at the inn door and in came Rodrigo Sforza.

"Are you the one who sends out magic horses?" Sforza asked boldly.

"What if I am?" Azzie asked.

"I've got one. I want a wish granted."

"It's not quite as easy as that," Azzie said. "There's some work you have to do first."

"I am quite prepared for that. But tell me, can you, will you, grant me my dearest wish?"

"Yes," Azzie said. "I can. What is it?"

"I want to be known far and wide as a scholar," Sforza said. "I want to be better known than Erasmus, and looked upon as a model of learning."

"Nothing simpler," Azzie said.

"I should mention that I can neither read nor write."

"That need not impede us."

"You're sure? I thought literacy was a prerequisite for great learning."

"So it is," Azzie said. "But what we are after here is the reputation, not necessarily the real thing. Listen carefully. You will have to undertake an adventure."

"Not a dangerous one, I hope."

"I hope not, either," Azzie said. "But first I have an errand to run. Wait for me here. I'll be back presently."

Azzie shed his cloak, freed his wings, and leaped into the sky with the sprite along to show the way.

Azzie found Mother Joanna at the bandits' camp. She and Hugh were seated at the table, going over a map and discussing what sounded like the hijacking of a caravan two days hence. As Azzie reached out to dismember a drunkenly merry man, she stayed his hand. "Hold, Azzie," she said. "These are my men. I am in charge here."

"What?" Azzie responded.

"My wish was granted even sooner than I'd anticipated," she stated. "For this I owe you considerable thanks."

"Think nothing of it," Azzie said. "Just be in Venice for the ceremony."

"Of course. And I do get to keep my soul?"

"Certainly. That was a part of the bargain."

"Good. I'll be there."

Shaking his head, Azzie sprang into the air and was gone.

PART NINE

Chapter 1

The first hint that the Hellenic gods had broken out of Afterglow en masse came at 013.32, Universal Sidereal Time, when the chief of Demonic Studies at Hell's Brimstonic University noted that one of his subalterns had failed to return from an expedition. The subaltern's assistant reported that a pack of loose deities had seized the researcher while he was poking around old bones at an archaeological dig near Mt. Olympus.

The chief called the Limbo underworld prison to see if anything had happened recently.

"Hello, who am I talking to?"

"Cicero, keeper of the Unwanted Deities Sector of the Limbo Life-Forms Penitentiary."

"I'm inquiring about the old gods of Greece. Zeus and that lot. Are they still safely under lock and key?"

"I'm sorry to say there's just been a breakout. They're free."

"When do you expect them to be rounded up?"

"I'm afraid it's not so easy. These old Greek gods are quite powerful, you know. It's going to take some action on Ananke's part to pen them up again."

"Thanks. I'll be in touch."

Chapter 2

"**B**ack in the real cosmos!" Phoebus cried.

"I could bend down and kiss the Earth," Hephaestus said.

The first thing they did was have a celebration, a reunion dinner roasting Zeus. They sang "For He's a Jolly Good Fellow"; they did comic imitations of his elaborate and portentous style. They sacrificed the usual animals and got the blood all over everything because servants, not the gods themselves, usually did the dirty work of sacrifice; they got drunk and acted in a bawdy fashion.

Zeus rapped on the table for attention. "I want to thank you all. It was very good of you to put on this celebration for me."

"Three cheers for Zeus!"

"Thank you. Thank you. Now then, on to something a bit more serious. I've been looking into what we might do with ourselves, now that we're out of Afterglow. I'm talking about all of us together."

"Do something together?" said Athena. "But we never do anything together!"

"We need to this time," Zeus said firmly. "Lack of cohesiveness is what brought on our defeat the last time. We're not going to make that mistake again! We need a project we can all work on, something that will serve our common good. It has come to my attention that the biggest thing going on now out there in the world is a certain play that a young demon of the modern persuasion is trying to mount for the edification of the world. This demon, Azzie Elbub, is planning to award seven players glorious prizes for no reason at all. Did you ever hear of such a thing?"

Zeus paused for comment. The gods and goddesses made none, but sat on their golden folding chairs and listened attentively.

Zeus went on. "The first thing we need to do is put a stop to this sort of vague and purposeless moralizing by upstart spiritual powers like the aforementioned demon. Didn't we ancient gods say that Character is Fate? Isn't that as true today as it ever was?"

"If we take action," Hermes said, "the Powers of Evil aren't going to like us putting the kibosh on their plans."

"I am indifferent to their feelings," Zeus replied. "If they don't like it, they know what they can do about it."

"But should we be getting into trouble so quickly?" said Hermes. "Wouldn't it be better to arbitrate? I'm sure we can find something to arbitrate. Meanwhile, perhaps we should lie low, or even hide."

"That would do no good at all," Zeus said. "The others, the Powers of Light and Dark, will try to put us back on the Limbo reservation. Anyway, where would we go? There's no place in the universe where we can hide. The powers that be are going to come for us sooner or later. Let's have some fun while we may, and strike a blow for our usual way of doing things—godlike trickery!"

They all cheered godlike trickery. It was a hallowed doctrine among them.

They gazed far out from Olympus and saw Sir Oliver's troop riding through some low hills.

"What's the story?" Athena asked as she and the others watched the great band of armed riders. Hordes of pilgrims, too, seemed to have joined the host.

"What happens when they reach Venice?" Hermes asked.

"Their leader gets what he most desires," Zeus told them. "Maybe, by extension, they do, too."

"Well, we can't have that happen, can we?" Athena demanded.

Zeus laughed and summoned the various wind gods, Zephyrus and Boreas among them. They whipped around Europe, Asia Minor, and parts of Asia collecting stray breezes. They stuffed these winds into a large leather bag and presented the bag to Zeus. Zeus loosened the leather thongs that held the mouth of the bag, and a west wind poked her head out and asked, "What's going on? Who goes around capturing wind?"

"We're Greek gods, and we capture winds when we please," said Zeus.

"Oh. Sorry I asked. What did you want us to do?"

"I'd like you to blow up a good storm."

The west wind looked more cheerful than before. "Oh, a storm! That's different! I thought you wanted one of those mild breezes people are always talking about."

"We don't care what people want," Zeus said. "We're gods and we want dramatic weather."

"Where do you want this storm?" the west wind asked, rubbing together her transparent hands.

"Ares," Zeus said, "why don't you go along with the winds and show them where we want them to blow? You could also direct the rain, while you're at it."

"Delighted," said Ares. "Especially since I consider weather to be war by other means."

Chapter
3

It was the worst weather that portion of Europe had seen in God knew how long. Storm clouds rose like swollen purple bladders blown up to monstrous proportions in the sky, and swept in filled with a rain that seemed to possess a living malevolence. The wind blew the lances out of men's hands. When the wind caught a shield from behind, it converted it into a sail, and if the holder of the shield happened to lose his balance it could blow him halfway across the countryside. Rain lashed at everything. Whipped by the wind into ultratiny drops driven with extraordinary force, it managed to penetrate every crack and crevice of armor or clothing.

Sir Oliver had to scream into his assistant's ear in order to be heard. "We'd better take shelter!"

"Aye, sir, it seems the only course. But how are we to pass the order? Who will hear us in this racket?"

"Something is amiss," Oliver said. "We'd better inform Antonio." For thus he still referred to Azzie.

"He's nowhere around, my lord."

"You must find him at once!"

"Yes, sir. But where?" The two men looked at each other, and then at the wide gray rain-soaked plain upon which they stood.

Chapter
4

Zeus wasn't content with simply serving up foul weather. He and all his children began working on separate schemes to let mankind know they were back.

Zeus left the company of the gods. He wanted to check out the human condition in its current state.

First he visited Greece. As he had feared, Greek strength of arms had slipped downhill badly since the grand old days of Agamemnon.

He looked around to see what other armies might be available. The rest of the forces of Western Europe were all engaged in one struggle or another. What he needed was a new force of men. He knew now just where he wanted to send them—barreling right down through the heart of Europe into Italy. He was going to start a new kingdom for himself there. His army would conquer, and they would make sure everyone worshiped him—or they would make war on those who did not. As their reward, he would deal them out glory and treachery. It was the old way, and the old way was always best, especially when it was bloody.

But first he had to find a pythoness who could tell him where there was an unoccupied army. A quick consultation of the Prophets' Directory helped him locate the Pythoness of Delphi, currently disguised as a washerwoman in a restaurant in Salonika.

● ● ●

In Salonika he withdrew the cloud of darkness into a large bladder and corked it so that it would be ready if he wanted to use it again. Then he went to the central agora and inquired for the washerwoman on the Main Baths. A fish merchant pointed the way. Zeus went past the ruined coliseum and the decayed horseracing ground, and there she was—a careworn old lady with her large tortoise shell that washerwomen used for wash buckets.

The pythoness had to take a disguise and do her prophesying in secret because the Church didn't allow pythonesses to continue in their familiar trade. Even owning a constrictor-type snake was against the law as "tending toward forbidden magical practices in the old outlawed style." But this pythoness still did private readings for friends and certain disaffected aristocrats.

Zeus went to her well wrapped in a cloak, but she recognized him at once.

"I need a reading," he told her.

"Oh, this is the finest day in my life," the pythoness said. "To think that I would ever meet one of the old gods face to face . . . Oh, just tell me what I can do for you."

"I want you to go into your trance and find out where I can get an army."

"Yes, sir. But since your son Phoebus is the god of prophecy, why don't you just ask him yourself?"

"I don't want to ask Phoebus or anybody like that," Zeus said. "I don't trust them. Surely there are other gods you ask questions of, not just us Olympians? What about that Jewish fellow who was around when I was?"

"Jehovah has gone through some interesting changes. But he's not available for prophesy. He left strict orders not to be disturbed."

"There are others, aren't there?"

"There are, of course, but I don't know if it's a good

idea to bother them with questions. They're not like you, Zeus, a god anyone can talk with. They're mean and they're strange."

"I don't care," Zeus said. "Ask them. If a god can't ask another god for a little advice, I don't know what the universe is coming to."

The pythoness took him to her chamber, lit the sacred laurel leaves, and piled on the sacred hemp. She took a few other sacred things and strewed them about, got her snake out of its wicker basket and wrapped it around her shoulders, and went into her trance.

Her eyes soon rolled back into her head, and she said, in a voice Zeus could not recognize but which set the hair on the back of his neck to rise, "O Zeus, go check out the Mongol peoples."

"Is there anything else?" Zeus asked.

The pythoness said, "End of message." And then she fainted.

After she had recovered, Zeus asked her, "I thought oracular answers were usually couched in strange and ambiguous terms. This one just came out and said what I was to do in a flat and straightforward manner. Has there been some change in operating procedure?"

"I believe," the pythoness said, "there's a general dissatisfaction in high circles with ambiguity. It wasn't getting anyone anywhere."

Zeus left Salonika wrapped again in his cloud of darkness, and turned to the northeast.

Chapter
5

Zeus visited the Mongols, who had recently conquered the southern Chinese empire. Viewing themselves as invincible, they were ripe to listen when Zeus came riding in.

Zeus found the Mongol chief at his headquarters.

"You and your men have done a fine thing, conquering this vast country, but now you lie around doing nothing. You are a people in search of a purpose, and I am a god in search of a people. What if we put our needs together and come up with something that will be good for us both?"

"You may be a god," Jagotai said, "but you're not our god. Why should I listen to you?"

"Because I'm offering to become your god," Zeus said. "I've about had it with the Greeks. An interesting and inventive people, but disappointing to a god who was only trying to bring them good things."

"What do you offer us?"

It soon came to pass that Mongol outriders, holding high their yak-tail banners, came riding hard through the Carpathian passes onto the flat plains of Friuli-Venezia Giulia, and riding through time into the sixteenth century. Zeus had to use all his powers to pull it off. It would have been easy to time-and-place-transport them directly, but it would have spooked the horses.

Panic spread through each resident population long before the Mongols arrived. The word was out everywhere —the Mongols were coming!

Whole families took themselves to horse, or to donkeys, or to oxcarts. The vast majority put what they could carry on their shoulders and streamed out in search of a place of refuge far from their pursuers, the flat-faced fiends with narrow black mustaches. Some people in their flight went to Milan, some to Ravenna. But for the most part, the refugees made for Venice, a city believed to be secure from invasion behind its marshes and lagoons.

Chapter 6

The Mongols were coming, and extraordinary measures were decreed to protect Venice. The Doge called a special session of the Council and laid certain proposals before it. It was agreed that the main bridges into the city proper should be cut; after that, the Venetians would raid the shores that surrounded them, confiscating all boats in the vicinity capable of carrying ten or more soldiers. These boats were to be taken up to the city itself, or sunk if they proved too heavy to carry away.

The problems of defense were rendered all the more complicated by a serious shortage of provisions. Normally, a constant stream of foodstuffs arrived daily on ships sailing from ports all over southeastern Europe and the Near East. But the recent storms had whipped the Mediterranean into a frenzy and put a halt to seaborne commerce. The city was already on short rations, and conditions promised to get worse.

The Venetians also faced a threat of widespread fires. People were trying to keep dry and warm, and they were often careless while lighting their stoves; the number of destructive fires in the city was greater than anyone had ever known before. Inevitably, there was talk that some had been set purposely, by agents of Venice's enemies; citizens were ordered to keep a close watch on strangers and to suspect the presence of spies in their midst at all times.

The rain came down in an incessant chatter that was like moist wind gods talking to each other with loose windows for tongues. Droplets dribbled off mantels and cornices and anything else that ended in a point. The wind drove the rain and broke big drops into little drops.

The water level rose steadily throughout Venice. Water overflowed the canals and flooded out into the squares and piazzas. It filled San Marco's Square to a depth of three feet, and it continued to rise. It was not the first time Venice had been bothered by rain and floods, but this was by far the worst anyone had seen.

Strong winds out of the northeast, laden with Arctic frost, blew steadily for days, and showed no signs of letting up. The republic's chief weather forecaster resigned his well-paid hereditary post, so distasteful had his work of predicting disaster become to him. People were praying to saints, devils, effigies, whatever they could think of, hoping to get some relief. Just to make matters worse, plague had been reported in some parts. And there were claims that Mongol outriders had been seen just a day's ride away, and there was no telling how quickly they were advancing.

The Venetians were exhausted by their constant worries, frightened by the huge forces shaping up outside of the republic, and suspicious even of each other. The usual ceremonies in honor of certain saints had fallen into abeyance. Churches were taken up day and night with prayers for the salvation of the city, and with anathemas delivered against the Mongols. Church bells tolled incessantly. This in turn spurred an air of desperate gaiety.

It was a brilliant season of parties, masked balls, and fetes. Carnival reigned constantly, and never had Venice shown herself to greater advantage. Despite the storms, candles gleamed brightly in the mansions of the rich, and music could be heard up and down the canals. People hurried through the rainswept streets in cloak and half mask, on their way from one party to the next. It was as if one last fling was all that remained for the proud old city.

It did not go unremarked that there was something extraordinary about what was occurring, something that seemed to surpass Earthly logic, something that smacked of the supernatural and of the coming of the last days. Astrologers searched through old parchment manuscripts and found predictions that the world was due to end soon, just as they had suspected, and that the Four Horsemen of the Apocalypse would soon be seen riding across the flaming sky at the time of the final sunset.

A strange incident occurred one day. A workman sent out by the city to assess storm damage discovered a hole in one of the dikes near the Arsenal. No water was coming through it, however. Through the opening there came a blinding yellow light, and the workman could see something indescribable in silhouette on the other side. It appeared to have two shadows. The man ran away and told others what he had seen.

A group of scholars came to study the phenomenon. The hole in the dike had grown larger; the brilliant yellow color had faded. Now the hole showed a clear and unearthly blue, even though stormy rain clouds and duncolored earth should have been visible through it. This hole was like an opening through everything, earth and sky alike.

The scholars studied it with trepidation. Little fragments of earth and sand on the edge of the hole were being pulled into it. As an experiment, they tossed a stray dog into the hole; the dog disappeared as soon as he broke the invisible plane of its surface.

One of the scholars said, "From a scientific point of view, this hole seems to be a rent or tear in the fabric of existence."

Another objected on a quibble. "How could the fabric of existence tear?"

"That we don't know," the first replied. "But we can infer that something tremendous is happening in the Spiritual Realm, something so enormous that it is having its effect on us down here on the physical plane of mundane existence. Not even reality is to be trusted any longer, so strange has life become."

More reports came in of other holes in the fabric of reality. The phenomenon was called the Anti-Imago, and examples of it seemed to be springing up everywhere, even in the interior chapel of San Marco's, where there was a hole almost three feet wide pointing obliquely downward and leading to where nobody could ascertain without taking the one-way trip into it.

A church sexton reported a peculiar occurrence. A stranger had entered the building, and something about him seemed either more or less than human. Perhaps it was his ears, or the strange tilt to his eyes. This being walked about the church and its immediate area, looking at outbuildings and making notes on a roll of parchment. When the sexton demanded to know what he was doing, the stranger said, "Just taking some measurements, so I can report the situation to the others."

"What others?"

"The others like me."

"But why should you and the others be interested in the state of our buildings?"

"We're provisional life-forms," the stranger said, "me and the others like me, so new we haven't even gotten a name yet. There's a chance we'll get to take over—reality, that is—and in that case we inherit what you leave behind. We thought it would be best to be prepared, so we are doing an inventory."

The report of this strange occurrence was investigated by learned doctors of the Church and judged to have never happened. The sexton's report was ascribed officially to an unaccountable hallucination. But this judgment came too late, the damage was done, people had heard and believed the story, and the sense of panic increased throughout the city.

Chapter 7

The pilgrims huddled in the common room in the inn, taking turns stoking the fire while they awaited their next orders. They should have been triumphant, happy, for they had finished their contest. But the weather trivialized their victories.

They had gone through hardships to get here, and now they were here and things were lousy. It wasn't the way it was meant to be. And none felt this more keenly than Azzie, who was being cheated of his story, though he couldn't figure out how it was happening.

That evening, as Azzie sat near the fire and tried to think what to do next, there was a rap at the inn door. The landlord called out, "We are full up, please go elsewhere!"

"You have someone within I would talk with," a pleasing female voice called out.

"Ylith!" Azzie called out. "Is that you?"

He gestured peremptorily to the landlord, who threw back the door with bad grace. A few bucketsful of rain blew in, and with them came a beautiful black-haired woman whose features were balanced between the angelic and the demonic, making her look very appealing indeed. She wore a simple yellow dress covered with appliquéd violets, and over it a sky blue cloak with a silver lining, a saucy red wimple about her head.

"Azzie!" she cried, crossing the room. "Are you all right?"

"Of course," Azzie said. "Your concern touches me. Have you perhaps changed your mind about a spot of dalliance?"

"Same old Azzie!" Ylith said with a chuckle. "I came here because I believe in fairness in all matters, especially those concerning Good and Bad. I think someone is doing you a disservice." Ylith then told how she had been captured by Hermes Trismegistus, who had given her to a mortal named Westfall. She told how she had been shut up in Pandora's box, and how with Zeus' help she had escaped.

"I know you think of Hermes as a friend," Ylith said, "but it seems he is plotting against you. The rest of the Olympians may be in on it, too."

"There's nothing much they can do from Afterglow," Azzie said.

"But the old gods are no longer in Afterglow. They've escaped! And I'm afraid I'm responsible, albeit unwittingly."

"It could be those guys who are screwing everything up," Azzie said. "I had thought it was all Michael's doing—you know how he opposes even my smallest triumph—but what's going on is beyond him. Someone has stirred up the Mongols, Ylith!"

"I don't understand why the Olympians are opposing you," Ylith said. "What difference does it make to them if you put on your immorality play?"

"The gods have a vested interest in morality," Azzie said. "But for others, not themselves. This interference of theirs is something else, I think. It wouldn't surprise me if this were the old gods' bid to return to power."

Chapter 8

The weather was simply no longer to be tolerated. Azzie roused himself and looked into it. The most cursory inspection showed him that the storms didn't seem to be coming from any single source. They sprang up "in the north," where the weather mostly comes from. But what did that mean, the north? How far north? North of what? And what was there in the north that created the weather? Azzie decided he had better find out, and do something about it if possible.

He explained to Aretino what he was going to do, and then went to the window and opened it. The blustery wind came in with a huff.

"This could be dangerous," Aretino said.

"Probably is," Azzie said, and, spreading his wings, he took to the air.

He left Venice and flew north, in search of the place where the weather came from. He traveled the length of Germany, and saw much bad weather, but it was all blowing in from even farther north. Azzie crossed the North Sea, touched on Sweden and found it was not the storm breeder, but merely a place storms passed over on their way to somewhere else. He veered into the eye of the wind and it took him toward Finland, where the Lapps had a great reputation as weather wizards. Wherever he went in that flat, snowy, pine-clad country, he always discovered that the weather didn't come "from here," it blew in "from over there," some place farther north.

At last he reached a region at the top of the world where the winds came funneling out at him with a speed and regularity that was impressive. The wind swept across the frozen tundra in a steady unending stream, and so strong was it that it resembled the waves of the sea more than rivers of the air.

Azzie pushed on, still moving to the north, though the whole world seemed to be narrowing and coming to a point here. He came at last to the very northernmost point of north and found a tall, narrow mountain of ice. On the top of that mountain was a tower, so old that it might have been put there before anything else existed and the only place was here.

The tower was topped by a platform, and on it stood a gigantic naked man with tangled hair and an expression most uncanny. He was working a large leather bellows. As he drove it up and down, the wind blew from its mouth. It was the origin of all the wind in the world.

The wind emerged from the bellows in a steady stream, and blew into and through the tubes of a peculiar-looking machine.

A strange creature sat in front of what looked like an organ keyboard, and his hands, with their many flexible fingers that almost appeared to be tentacles, played on the keys and shaped and formed the winds that passed through them. It was an allegorical machine, such as religions produce when they are trying to explain how things work. It directed the shaped and conditioned winds produced by the bellows pumper to the window, where they began their journey south to all points of the globe, and especially to Venice.

But why Venice? Azzie focused his X-ray vision,

which all demons have but few use because it's difficult to work, like trying to do long division in your head. But now that he looked, Azzie could see that Ley lines had been drawn on the land beneath the ice, and these lines guided the winds and augmented their ferocity.

But what about the rain? Everything here in the topmost reaches of the north was dry, crisp, and brand-spanking-new, and without a trace of moisture.

Azzie looked around, but he saw no one but the man working the bellows and the other one, the operator of the wind machine. He said to them both, "My dear sirs, you are screwing things up in the portion of Earth where I reside, and I cannot permit it. I intend to do something about it unless you cease and desist upon the instant."

He had spoken up bravely, and he had no idea if he could prevail against these two strange creatures. But it was in his nature to advance boldly, and his nature did not desert him now.

The two creatures introduced themselves. They were incarnations of the god Baal. The one working the bellows was Baal-Hadad, the other was Baal-Quarnain, Canaanite deities who had been living quietly for some thousands of years, since the last of their worshipers had died. Zeus had enlisted them both into his service, saying there were none better for bringing up the sort of weather he was interested in, once the initial bag of breezes had been exhausted. Zeus himself was a weather god, but he was too busy nowadays for the tedious work of making weather.

The old Canaanite deities, despite their glossy black wavy hair, hooked noses, prominent eyes, and bold features, despite their swarthy skin and huge hands and feet, were timid deities. When Azzie told them he was angry, and ready to call down a lot of trouble on their heads, both were willing to desist.

"We can stop the wind," said Baal-Hadad, "but the rain isn't up to us. We have nothing to do with it. All we send out of here is pure wind."

"Do you know who's sending the rain?" Azzie asked. They both shrugged.

"Then it'll wait," Azzie said. "I have to get back. It's about time for the ceremony."

Chapter 9

Aretino made sure all was in readiness at the inn. Then he went up to Azzie's room.

Azzie wore a green dressing gown with golden dragons embroidered over it. He was seated at a table and bent over a parchment, a quill pen in his hand. He did not even look up. "Come in," he said.

Aretino entered. "Not dressed yet? My dear lord demon, the ceremony is soon to begin."

"Plenty of time," Azzie said. "I'm a bit winded, and my outfit is all laid out in the other room. Come help me, Aretino. I have to decide who to award prizes to. First, is everyone present?"

"They're all here," Aretino said, and poured himself a glass of wine. He was feeling very good. This play was going to send his already great reputation sky-high. He would be more famous than Dante, better known than Virgil, maybe even surpass Homer. It was the high moment of his life, and he suspected no trouble when there came a knock at the door.

It was an imp messenger from Ananke. "She wants you," the messenger said. "And she's mad."

The Palace of Justice, where Ananke held sway, was a Brobdingnagian place sculpted from blocks of stone larger than entire pyramids on Earth. Despite its size, the Palace was built with classic proportions observed entirely throughout. The columns in front were thicker than a gaggle of elephants. The grounds were beautifully landscaped, too. On the well-trimmed lawn, sitting on a red-checked blanket near a white gazebo, with a tea service spread out around her, was Ananke.

This time there was no question what she looked like. It is known that Ananke can take many forms. One of those forms, the Indescribable, is the one she takes when she wants to discourage flatterers. It is a mode of being that literally resists description. The most one can say is that Ananke looked nothing like a steam shovel. She had chosen this mode of appearance for the occasion.

As soon as Azzie was in her presence, Ananke said to him, "Too much with the magic horses already!"

"What do you mean?" Azzie said.

"You were warned, boychick," Ananke said. "Magic is not a panacea for all that ails your ambition. You can't use magic to solve everything. It is against the nature of things to assume that matters can go in any but their customary ways whenever you please to ask them to."

"I've never seen you in a state like this," Azzie said.

"You'd be mad, too, if you saw the entire cosmos threatened."

"But how did that happen?" Azzie asked.

"It was the magic horses," Ananke said. "Magic candlesticks were all right, but when you invoked magic horses, too, you simply stretched the fabric of credulity too far."

"What do you mean, the fabric of credulity?" Azzie asked. "I've never heard you talk like this."

"Tell him, Otto," Ananke said.

Otto, a spirit who for reasons known best to himself wears the disguise of a fat middle-aged German with a heavy white mustache and thick glasses, stepped out from behind a tree.

"Do you think the universe can stand an endless amount of tampering?" he asked. "You've been playing with the meta-machinery, whether you know it or not. You've been throwing a spanner in the works."

"He doesn't seem to understand," Ananke said.

"Is something going wrong?" Azzie asked.

"*Ja,* something's going wrong with the very nature of things," Otto said.

"The nature of things? Surely it's not as bad as all that?"

"You heard me. The structure of the universe has become deranged, due in no small measure to you and your magic horses. I know what I'm talking about. I've been servicing this universe since time out of mind."

"I never heard of a maintenance man for the universe," Azzie said.

"Stands to reason, don't it? If you're going to have a universe at all, you need someone to take care of it, and that can't be the one who runs it. She has a lot of other stuff to do, and maintenance is a specialty in itself and doesn't need to be connected with anything else. You did bring in those magic horses, didn't you?"

"I suppose I did," Azzie said, "but what of it, what's wrong with magic horses?"

"You used too many of them, that's what's wrong. Do you really expect you can clutter up the landscape with all the magic horses you want to use? All to provide easy explanations for stuff you're too lazy to work out beforehand? No, my fine young demon, you've gone and messed up this time. This damned universe is changing under our eyes, after all my years of holding it together, and there's nothing you or Ananke or me or anyone else can do about it. You've loosed the lightning of His terrible swift sword, if you take my meaning, and now there's going to be Hell to pay in the Badlands. You've toyed with reality one time too often."

"What does this have to do with reality?" Azzie asked.

"Listen up good now, my fine young demon. Reality is a sphere of solid matter made up of various substances lying in strata. Where one stratum abuts another, there, we can say, is a potential fault line, just as it is in the Earth. Anomalies are the things that explode shock waves along these interfaces. Your illicit use of the magic horses was one such anomaly bomb. But other anomalous things have been happening, too. The fact that the old gods have escaped is an event so impossible that its occurrence has shaken the universe.

"It is poor Venice that is bearing the brunt of this cosmic disaster that you have perpetrated. The city has had the bad luck to be the focus of events, and your work has subjected it to a reality strain. The floods, the Mongol invasion, and the plague soon to follow, are not at all part of the main line of Venetian history. They weren't really supposed to happen at all. They are side possibilities, with vanishingly small chances of being activated in the normal run of things. But due to you they have been activated, and so all of recorded history from this time forward lies under threat of destruction."

"How can time forward be threatened?" Azzie asked.

"You must think of the future as something that has already happened, and that is threatening to happen again, wiping out all that has gone before. That is what we must avoid at all costs."

"A lot of stuff is going to come down," Ananke said. "But first, you must get these pilgrims of yours back to their homes."

Azzie had to be content with that. But at the back of

his mind, there began a small stirring beneath the sea of anxiety. Ananke said he wasn't acting according to reality. But what was reality but the balance, the agreement, between Good and Bad? If he could get Michael to change that agreement, to their mutual benefit . . . But first he had to look in on his pilgrims.

PART TEN

Chapter 1

When Azzie left the Palace of Justice his tail was between his legs and a suspicious wetness was in the corners of his brown eyes. He was trying to get used to the idea that his play, his great immorality play that was going to astonish the worlds, was never going to happen. The legend, the all-important legend of the golden candlesticks, was not to be allowed to play to its ending. He was under direct and unambiguous orders from Ananke Herself to stop his actors in midscene.

There had to be a way around her order. Moodily he went to a Power Booth outside the Palace of Justice and refilled his travel spell. At a nearby lunch area he found a stall that specialized in quick convenience foods for demons, where he bought a sack of deviled cats' heads in a nice clotted red sauce. It would give him something to snack on on his way back to Earth. Then he activated his spell and found himself hurtling through the transparent veils that spiritual space seems composed of.

As he flew, he munched on the cats' heads and thought furiously. Despite his utmost efforts at transcendental casuistry, he could find no way to get around Ananke's command without her finding out sooner or later and coming down hard on him. And it wasn't just Ananke that he had to fear. There was also the fact that he had upset the balance of the cosmos by his overuse of magic horses. Were he to persist, it might all fall apart, the whole shooting match, everything, all of creation, engulfed in the pure white flame of self-contradiction. If that happened, the cosmos itself might collapse. At the very least, the laws of reason would be overturned.

Soon he was back over Venice, and the sight of the city from the air was a sad one. Rising waters had already engulfed some of the low-lying outer islands. The winds had fallen off, but floodwaters had risen to engulf the San Marco's Square to a depth of ten feet. The older and less secure buildings were already collapsing as the brackish tidal waters washed out the old mortar that held their bricks and stones together.

Azzie came down at Aretino's house and found the poet outside in his shirtsleeves, trying to shore up his house with sandbags. It was a task useless on the face of it, and Aretino put down his tools and sadly followed Azzie indoors.

They found a dry room on the second floor. Wasting no time, Azzie said, "Where are the pilgrims now?"

"They're still at the inn."

Now Azzie had to change the plans, collect all the golden candlesticks, and make sure they got back to Fatus' castle in Limbo. Then he needed to get the pilgrims out of Venice. He saw no reason, however, to tell Aretino all of that just now. He would find out when the others did that the ceremony had been scrubbed.

"We're going to have to get the pilgrims out of Venice," Azzie told Aretino. "Between the Mongols and the floods, this city looks doomed. I have it on good authority that there's going to be a change in the timeline in which this sequence of world history is taking place."

"A change? What do you mean?"

"The world spins a timeline, and from it different events spring forth. The way things are going now, Venice looks as if it will be destroyed. But this result is unacceptable to Ananke, so the Venice timeline will be split just before I started with the golden candlesticks. It will become the new main line. This line, the one we're in now, will be relegated to Limbo."

"And what will that mean?" Aretino asked.

"The Limbo version of Venice will run for no longer than a week, from the time I first asked you to write a play to the time, predicted for midnight tonight, when the Mongols arrive and the floods spill over the walls. It will have but a week of life, in one sense, but that week will replay itself, beginning again as soon as it has reached its end. The inhabitants of the Limbo version of Venice will have an eternity of weeks, each of which will end in doom and destruction."

"But if we get the pilgrims away from Venice?"

"If we get them out before midnight they will be able to continue their normal lives, exactly as if I had never happened. They will be returned to the time just before they met me."

"Will they have any memory of what happened?"

Azzie shook his head. "Only you will remember, Pietro. I'm arranging that so you can write the play based on our contest."

"I see," Aretino said. "Well, it's all a little unexpected. I don't know how they'll like it."

"They don't have to like it," Azzie said. "They just have to do it. Or suffer the consequences if they don't."

"I'll make sure they understand that."

"Do so, most excellent Pietro. I'll meet you at the church."

"Where are you going?"

"I've got one more idea," Azzie said, "that just might save this whole thing."

Chapter
2

Azzie passed quickly into the Ptolemaic system with its crystal spheres and stars fixed in their orbits. It always cheered him to see the orderly recession of the stars and the fixed planes of existence. He hurried on until he reached the Visitors' Gate that lets into Heaven. This is the only entrance that visitors are supposed to use, and there are severe penalties for anyone, human or demon, trying to enter by any of the angels' gates.

The Visitors' Gate was a literal gate of bronze, a hundred feet high and set in marble. The approach to it was thick with fleecy little white clouds, and angelic voices in the air sang songs of hallelujah. In front of the gate were a table and chair made of mahogany, and seated at the table was a balding oldish man with a long white beard, dressed in a white satin sheet. He wore a name tag that read, ST. ZACHARIAS AT YOUR SERVICE. HAVE A HOLY DAY. Azzie didn't know him. But usually it was one of the lesser saints who pulled this duty.

"What can I do for you?" Zacharias asked.

"I need to see Michael the Archangel."

"Did he leave your name on the visitors' list?"

"I doubt it. He didn't know I was coming."

"In that case, my dear sir, I'm very much afraid—"

"Look," Azzie said, "this is an urgent matter. Just send my name in to him. He'll thank you for it."

Grumbling, St. Zacharias went to a golden speaking tube that snaked down the side of the bronze door. He said a few words into it and waited, humming to himself. Then someone spoke through the other end.

"You're sure? It's not really proper form . . . Yes . . . Of course, sir.

"You're to go in," Zacharias said. He opened a small wooden door set in the base of the big bronze door. Azzie went inside, past the scattered buildings that were set out on the green lawn of Heaven. Soon he was at the office building in West Heaven, and Michael was standing on the steps waiting for him.

Michael ushered Azzie into his office. He poured him a glass of wine. Heaven has the finest wine, though for good whiskey you need to go to Hell. They chatted a while. Then Michael asked him what he wanted.

"I want to make a deal," Azzie said.

"A deal? What kind of a deal?"

"Did you know that Ananke has ordered me to stop my immorality play?"

Michael looked at him, then grinned. "She has, has she? Good old Ananke!"

"Do you think so?" Azzie said frigidly.

"Indeed I do," Michael said. "Although she's supposed to be above Good and Bad, and indifferent to both, yet I'm glad to see she knows which side her morality is buttered on."

"I want to make a deal," Azzie repeated.

"You want my help in opposing Ananke?"

"That's exactly it," Azzie said.

"You astound me. Why should I make a deal with you? Ananke is stopping you from putting on your immorality play. That's just the way I like it!"

"Is this the sound of personal pique I hear?" Azzie asked.

Michael smiled. "Oh, perhaps a little. I do get annoyed at your carryings-on. But my decision to stop your play is not based on personalities. It is an advantage to my side to stop this insidious play you want to mount. It's as simple as that."

"You may find it amusing," Azzie said, "but it's a more serious matter than you've given it credit for."

"Serious for whom?"

"For you, of course."

"How could that be? She's doing what we want."

"The fact that she is doing anything is the bad news," Azzie said.

Michael sat up straight. "How do you figure?"

"Since when has Ananke ever concerned herself with the daily operations of our struggle, yours and mine, between Dark and Light?"

"This is the first time I can ever remember her interfering directly," Michael admitted. "What are you getting at?"

"Do you accept Ananke as your ruler?" Azzie demanded.

"Of course not! She has nothing to do with the decisions of Good or Bad. Her part in the running of the cosmos is to set an example, not to make law."

"Yet here she is, making law," Azzie said. "Forbidding me to put on a play."

Michael smiled. "I can't get too serious about that!"

"You could if it were your play that was being stopped."

Michael's smile faded. "But it's not."

"Not this time. But if you accept the precedent that Ananke can set rules for Bad, how are you going to argue when she sets a rule for Good?"

Michael scowled. He stood up and paced rapidly up and down the room. At last he stopped and turned to Azzie.

"You're right. Her stopping your play, blessing though it is to us who are opposed to you, is nevertheless overstepping the rules that govern all of us. How dare she?"

Just then the doorbell chimed. Michael gestured impatiently and it swung open.

"Babriel! Good! I was just about to send for you!"

"I have brought you a message," Babriel said.

"It will have to wait," Michael said. "I have just learned that Ananke is poaching on our preserve, so to speak. I'll need to speak to Gabriel and some of the others immediately."

"Yes, sir. They want to speak to you, too."

"They do?"

"That's why they sent the message, sir."

"They did? But what do they want?"

"They didn't tell me, sir."

"Wait here," Michael said.

"You mean me?" Babriel asked.

"Both of you." He strode out of the room.

Soon Michael returned. He was subdued, and he didn't meet Azzie's eye.

"I'm afraid I'm not going to be allowed to interfere in this matter regarding Ananke."

"But what about the point I made? About the potential abrogation of your own power?"

"I'm afraid that is not the main concern," Michael said.

"Then what is?"

"The preservation of the cosmos," Michael said. "That's what's at stake, the Supreme Council tells me."

"Michael, there's a matter of freedom involved here," said Azzie. "The freedom of Good and Bad to act according to the dictates of their reason, held back only by natural law, not by the arbitrary rule of Ananke."

"I don't like it either," Michael said. "But there it is. Give up your play, Azzie. You're outgunned and overruled. I doubt if even your own Council of Evil would back you in this."

"We'll just see about it," Azzie said, and he made a striking exit.

Chapter 3

The pilgrims were still inside the inn when Azzie returned to Venice. Rodrigo and Cressilda sat together in one corner; although they weren't talking to one another, each was the only person of sufficient rank for the other to be comfortable with. As usual, Kornglow and Leonore were oblivious to everyone else. Puss and Quentin played cat's cradle with a bit of string. Mother Joanna tended to a bit of knitting, while Sir Oliver put a high polish on the jeweled hilt of his ceremonial sword, the one he intended to wear for the ceremony.

Azzie began briskly enough. "I'm afraid we've got a bit of trouble. Our play has been canceled. But let me thank you for all the work you've done. You've all handled your candlesticks extremely well."

Sir Oliver said, "Antonio, what is happening? Are we to get our wishes or not? I have my acceptance speech all ready. We need to begin."

The others piped in with their remonstrances. Azzie silenced them with a gesture.

"I don't know how to tell you this, but the highest possible source has commanded me to strike this production. There'll be no ceremony of the golden candlesticks."

"But what's gone wrong?" Mother Joanna asked.

"It seems we've broken some silly old natural law."

Mother Joanna looked puzzled. "But people break natural laws all the time. What of it?"

"Usually, it doesn't matter at all," Azzie said. "This time, though, I'm afraid we've been caught out. I'm told that my use of the magic horses was overzealous."

"Surely all that can be taken care of later," Sir Oliver said. "For now, we're eager to go on."

"And I am eager to have you do so," Azzie said. "But alas, it cannot be. Aretino will now pass among you and gather up the candlesticks."

Sullenly Aretino walked among them, accepting the candlesticks they reluctantly handed over.

"We're going to have to get out of here," Azzie said. "Venice is doomed. We must leave at once."

"So soon?" said Mother Joanna. "I haven't even started visiting the famous shrines."

"If you don't want this place to be your shrine, you'll do as I say," Azzie said. "You must all follow Aretino. Pietro, do you hear? We must get these people off the islands of Venice!"

"Easier said than done," Aretino grumbled. "But I'll do what I can."

He put the stacked candlesticks in a corner near the altar. "Now what do you want me to do with them?"

Azzie was about to answer when he felt a tug at his sleeve. He looked down. It was Quentin, with Puss beside him.

"Please, sir," said Quentin, "I've learned all my lines to say for this ceremony. Puss and I thought them up together, and we both learned them."

"That's very nice, children," Azzie said.

"Won't we get a chance to say them?" Quentin asked.

"You can tell your lines to me later, when I've gotten you safe away from Venice."

"But sir, that won't be the same thing. We learned them for the ceremony."

Azzie grimaced. "There isn't going to be any ceremony."

"Did one of us do something bad?" Quentin asked.

"No, it's nothing like that," Azzie said.

"Was it a bad play, then?"

"No!" Azzie cried. "It was not a bad play! It was a fine play! All of you were acting just like yourselves, and that's the best acting job possible."

"If it wasn't a bad play," Quentin said, "and we didn't do anything wrong, why can't we finish it?"

Azzie opened his mouth to speak, but he hesitated. He was remembering himself as a young demon, contemptuous of all authority, willing to pursue his sin and his virtue, his pride and his will, to wherever they would lead him. Well, he had changed a lot since that day. Now a mere woman commanded him, and he obeyed. It was true that Ananke wasn't quite the same as a woman—she was more like a vague but compelling divine principle with breasts. She had always loomed above everything, compelling but remote. But here she was, breaking the precedent that had been set since the beginning of time not to interfere. And who did she pick to be the bearer of her broken precedent? Azzie Elbub.

"My dear child," Azzie said, "to go on with this ceremony could mean the death of us all."

"I guess we all have to die someday, sir," Quentin said. Azzie stared at him, because the lad had the effrontery of a demon and the sangfroid of a saint. Could Azzie do any less?

"All right, kid," he said. "You've talked me into it. Everybody! Pick up your candlesticks and take your places on the stage that has been set up in front of the bar!"

"You're going through with it!" Aretino cried joyfully. "I am very thankful, sir. For what ending would I have had otherwise for the play I intend to write from this material?"

"You've got something to write about now," Azzie said. "Is the orchestra in the pit?"

They were, still cheerful because Aretino had paid them triple their usual wage to hang around waiting for Azzie, and because the city was so flooded that there were no other musical performances planned.

The orchestra struck up a tune. Azzie waved his hand. The ceremony began.

Chapter 4

The ceremony was all pomp and circumstance such as demons and Renaissance people loved. Unfortunately there was no visible audience; this had to be a private affair. But it was all very impressive, there in the otherwise deserted inn, with the rain hammering overhead.

The pilgrims marched through the room, all dressed in their holiday best. They bore their candlesticks, which they retrieved from Aretino. They marched down the aisle and mounted to the stage. Azzie, master of ceremonies now, introduced each one, and made a short complimentary speech about him or her.

Eerie things began happening. There was a strange popping of curtains. The wind took on an uncanny moan. A pungent, unearthly smell suffused the space. Most prominent was a wind that sounded like a tormented soul trying to get in.

"I've never heard the wind sound like that," Aretino said.

"It's not the wind," Azzie said.

"I beg your pardon?"

But Azzie refused to elaborate. He knew a visitation when he heard one. He had presided at too many to be deceived now, when an unearthly chill seemed to settle on the building, and curious thumping noises came from all over.

Azzie only hoped this new force, whatever it was, would hold off making an appearance for a while. It seemed to be having difficulty finding its way. And the Hell of it was, Azzie didn't even know who or what was hunting for him. It was an unusual situation, a demon being haunted by what seemed to be a ghost. Azzie got an idea of what lay ahead then, the vast chasms of unreason that threatened now to engulf those fragile edifices, logic and causality. With just the tiniest movement, it seemed, those things might cease to be.

After the speeches came a short, tasteful interlude that featured singing by the local boys' choir, an all-Europe-class group that Aretino had booked for this occasion. Some thought St. Gregory himself was putting in a ghostly appearance, for a tall thin shape had begun to materialize near the door. But whatever it was hadn't quite got it right; it faded out before it could fully materialize itself, and the ceremony was able to continue.

Next, the contestants massed their candlesticks on the altar and lit them. Azzie made a short speech congratulating his contestants, driving home the premise of his play by pointing out that they had done well by simply going about their natural pursuits. They had won good fortune through no great effort, and that good fortune was by no means the concomitant of good character and good action. On the contrary, good luck was a neutral quality that could happen to anyone. "As proof of that," Azzie said, "here stand my contestants, all of whom have earned golden rewards this evening by nothing more taxing than being themselves in all their imperfections."

Throughout all of this Aretino sat in a front-row pew and was busy scribbling notes. He was already planning out the play he would weave from this material. It was all very well for Azzie to think it was sufficient to stage a sort of divine comedy, but that was not the way of art. The really good stuff was contrived, not improvised, and that was what Aretino planned to do with it.

Aretino was so busy writing that he didn't realize the ceremony was over until the pilgrims were all around him, pounding him on the back and asking if he'd liked their speeches. Aretino curbed his natural acerbity and declared that they all had done well.

"And now," Azzie said, "it's time to get out of here. You won't need your candlesticks any longer. Just pile them in the corner there and I'll call up a minor miracle to get them back to Limbo. Aretino, are you ready to lead these people to safety?"

"Indeed I am," Aretino said. "If it's possible to get off this island, I'll find a way. Are you not going to accompany us?"

"I intend to," Azzie said, "but I may be delayed along the way by circumstances beyond my control. If that should happen, you know what to do, Pietro. Get these people to safety!"

"And what of you?"

"I'll do what I can to keep myself alive," Azzie said. "Perseverance in our own self-interests is a faculty highly developed in us demons."

Azzie, Aretino, and the little troop of pilgrims went forth into the stormy night of the doom that was falling upon Venice.

Chapter 5

They left the inn and hurried out into the storm. The streets were filled with people trying to flee the city; the water was now waist high and still rising. Aretino had brought along plenty of bribe money, but he could find no available boatmen to bribe. The various stations along the Grand Canal had been abandoned hours ago.

"I don't know what to do," Aretino told Azzie. "Every boat in the city seems to be destroyed or already booked."

"There's still a way of getting the contestants to safety," Azzie said. "It will no doubt result in another anomaly for which I'll be held to blame, but we'll try it anyway. We need to find Charon. His boat is always around places like this where there are so many dead and dying. He's a connoisseur of large-scale tragedies."

"The actual Charon from the Greek myths is here?"

"Certainly. Somehow he's been able to continue ferrying people all through the Christian era. That's an anomaly too, but one they can't blame on me."

"Will he take living people? I thought Charon's boat was only for the other kind."

"I know him pretty well. We've done business together. I think he'll make an exception, this being an emergency of the sort he likes."

"Where do we find him?"

Azzie led them in the right direction. Aretino wanted to know what the big hurry was to get the pilgrims off. "Is the situation really so bad?" he asked.

"Yes, it is. The fall of Venice is only the beginning; it heralds the collapse of the entire universe. Both the Copernican and the Ptolemaic models are in difficulty, and the signs of anomaly shock are everywhere. Already the streets are full of prodigies and miracles. Business has come to a standstill, and even love has been forced to put itself on hold."

"I don't understand," Aretino said. "What is this anomaly explosion? What is going to happen? How will this catastrophe reveal itself? By what signs will it be known?"

"You will know it beyond doubt," Azzie said. "There will be a sudden discontinuity in the action of life. Causes and effects will no longer add up. Conclusions will no longer flow sweetly from their premises. As I told you, reality will fork into two branches. One branch will go on with the story of Europe and the Earth as if this pilgrimage had never taken place, while the other will continue what is going on now, bringing the results of the pilgrimage. It is that branch, that disaster, that will be sent to Limbo. There it will repeat itself over and over, in a loop bigger than all outdoors. We need to get the pilgrims out before that happens."

But Charon was not to be found. Aretino and Azzie carried on, shepherding their pilgrims from one point to another, hoping to find a way to get them out. Some people were already trying to swim to the mainland and were drowning, many of them pulled under by other struggling swimmers.

The few remaining gondoliers were already occupied with passengers. Those lucky enough to have gotten aboard

had drawn their swords, and with these they menaced anyone who approached them.

Azzie and Aretino searched up and down the narrow
winding streets, looking for Charon. At last they found his
boat, slab sided and misshapen, and painted a matte black.
Azzie walked up to the snuff-colored rail, put one narrow
foot upon it, and called out, "Ho, boatman!"

A tall, skinny old man with sunken jaws and preternaturally bright eyes came out from the little cabin into the
torchlight. "Azzie!" he said. "You do pop up in some
strange places!"

"What are you doing in Venice, Charon, so far from
your usual route on the Styx?"

"We boatmen of the dead have been commanded to
extend service to the area. I have it on good authority that
there's going to be a die-off here like nothing anyone has
seen since Atlantis foundered."

"I'd like to hire your services now."

"Is it really necessary? I was going to get a little sleep
before the big evacuation begins."

"This whole construct is in a lot of trouble," Azzie said.
"I need your help to get my friends out of here."

"I don't help anyone," Charon said. "I have my own
rounds. There are plenty of deceased people still to ferry to
the land of the dead."

"You don't seem to appreciate the seriousness of the
position."

"It's not serious for me," Charon said. "However death
comes, that's a matter for the Upper World. In the Kingdom of the Dead, all is serene."

"That's what I'm trying to get across to you. It's not
going to be that way for long, not even in the Kingdom of
the Dead. Didn't it ever occur to you that even Death can
die?"

"Death die? What a ridiculous notion!"

"My dear fellow, if God can die, then Death can die, too, and very painfully. I'm trying to tell you the whole construct is in trouble. You could be wiped away along with everything else."

Charon was skeptical, but he allowed himself to be convinced. "What is it you want done?"

"I must get the pilgrims out of here and restore them to their starting places. Only with that done will Ananke have a chance to get everything back to normal again."

Charon was capable of moving with speed when he wanted to. Once the pilgrims were aboard he directed the boat, standing at the rear with the tiller under his arm, a cloaked scarecrow figure. The crazy old boat picked up speed, powered by the arms of the dead rowers who sat out of sight in the hold. Fires burned on all sides in the beleaguered city, shooting ghastly reds and yellows up into the blue-black skies. The boat crossed the arm of the bay, and soon they were gliding through reeds and marshes. Everything looked strange; Charon had taken a shortcut through a watery connection that joined one world to another. "Is this how it was at the beginning?" Aretino asked.

"I wasn't there right at the beginning," Charon told him, "but close to it. This is how the world looked when there was no physical law and all was magic. There was a time before everything, when magic ruled, when reason was not. We visit it still in our dreams, that world of long ago. Certain landscapes elicit memories of that world. It is of the place older than God, older than creation. The world before the creation of the universe."

.   .   .

In the stern, Aretino had been going over the list of pilgrims to make sure they were all accounted for. He soon found two or three wily Venetians who had taken advantage of the general confusion to get a ride to the mainland. That was all right; there was enough room for a few more, especially since Kornglow and Leonore were nowhere to be found.

Aretino asked if anyone had seen them. No one had since the ceremony with the candlesticks.

Everyone else was aboard the boat—everyone except Azzie, who stood on the pier and unfastened the ship's line.

"I can't find Kornglow or Leonore!" Aretino called to Azzie.

"We can't wait any longer!" Charon said. "Death keeps to a strict schedule."

"Go ahead without them," Azzie said.

"But what about you?" Aretino asked.

"There is that which will detain me," Azzie said. It was then that Aretino noticed the shadow at Azzie's back, which seemed to be gripping him by the neck.

Azzie threw the line aboard. Charon's houseboat moved away from the shore and began to gain way as the oars of the dead dipped into the waters.

"Is there nothing we can do for you?" Aretino called out.

"No!" Azzie replied. "Just keep going. Get away from here!"

He watched the houseboat glide into the shadowy waters until it vanished among reeds and marshes near to the other shore.

The pilgrims made themselves as comfortable as they could, crowded in among dead rowers who were not the most congenial companions.

"Hello," Puss said to the gaunt cowled figure who sat on the bench beside her.

"Hello, little lady," answered that individual. It was a woman. She appeared to be dead, even though she was still somehow able to talk.

"Where are you going?" Puss asked.

"Our boatman Charon is taking us to Hell," the cowled figure said.

"Oh! I'm so sorry!" Puss said.

"No need to grieve," the figure said. "That's where it all winds up."

"Even me?" said Puss.

"Even you. But you needn't worry, it won't take place for quite some time."

Quentin, on the other side, asked, "Is there anything to eat on this boat?"

"Nothing good," the cowled figure replied. "What we have is bitter."

"I'd really like something sweet," Quentin said.

"Be patient," Puss said. "Nobody gets to eat on the boat of the dead without forfeiting their lives. I think I see the shore ahead."

"Oh, all right," Quentin said. He wished he were still acting as messenger to the spirits. That had been fun.

PART ELEVEN

Chapter
1

Venice seemed doomed now. There might be a way Azzie could still save it, though. He would have to go to the Backstage Universe where the Cosmic Machinery was stored—in that part of the cosmos where symbology rules.

To get there he would need to follow a set of instructions he had never used before—instructions he had thought he would never have to use. But now was the time. He found a sheltered place under a balustrade and made a complex gesture.

A disembodied voice—one of the Guardians of the Way—said to him, "Are you sure you want to do this?"

"I am," Azzie said.

And disappeared . . .

Azzie reappeared in a small waiting room. There was a long padded sofa against one wall, two chairs on the other. A big lamp cast a mellow glow over a stack of magazines on a nearby end table. Before the third wall was a receptionist, clad in a toga, sitting in front of what looked like an office intercom. The receptionist looked for all the world like a woman, except that she had an alligator's head on her shoulders. The sight of her convinced Azzie that he was indeed in the place where realism held no sway and where symbology ruled the world.

"What can we do for you, sir?" the receptionist asked.

"I'm here to inspect the symbolic machinery," Azzie said.

"Go right in. You were expected."

Azzie passed through a door into a space that had the dismaying qualities of being both enclosed and endless, a universal plenum filled with innumerable contents. It seemed to be a factory, or a derisive three-dimensional comment on one, for its volume was interminable to the eye. This place beyond space and time seemed entirely filled with machinery, with an endless variety of cogwheels and spindles, with belts to drive them, all of them apparently suspended in midair and working away with a zinging, hissing, clanging sound.

The machines were piled up endlessly in all directions, separated by narrow catwalks. On one of these catwalks was a tall, gaunt man, wearing gray coveralls with a thin white stripe and a peaked cap of a similar material. He moved along with his oilcan, making sure the machinery ran with a minimum of friction.

"What's going on here?" Azzie asked.

"Here all of Earth's time is compressed into a single narrow strip and passed through rollers. And it comes out here, a broad gossamer-thin tapestry."

The old man showed him the broad rollers where the timelines were woven into a tapestry that represented and in some sense was the history of the cosmos up to that moment. Azzie examined it and found a botched place.

"What about this?" he asked.

"Ah, that's where Venice was destroyed," the old man said. "The city was one of the principal threads in the fabric of civilization, you see, and so there'll be a bit of a discontinuity in the cultural aspect of the space-time fabric until another city takes up its place. Or perhaps the whole tapestry will lose luster for loss of one of its finest parts. It's difficult to predict the effect of a major fallout like this."

"Seems a pity to leave it at that," Azzie said. He examined the threads that made up the warp. "Look, if we go back and pull out this one strand, Venice would be all right."

He had found the strand where he had begun his golden candlestick game with the pilgrims, the point at which Venice's doom had been sealed. It was necessary to withdraw that action from the skein of causality in order to undo the cosmic damage.

"My dear young demon, you know very well we can't mess with the skeins of time. I agree it would be easy. But I would not recommend it."

"What if I did it anyhow?"

"Try it and find out."

"Are you going to stop me?"

The old man shook his head. "My duty is not to stop anything. My task is solely to watch the spinning of the tapestry."

Azzie reached out and with a firm motion pulled out the thread that marked his meeting with the pilgrims. The thread lit with sudden fire as it tore loose. He could see the result immediately on the slow-moving web of tapestry, which repaired itself at once. Venice was restored. It was as easy as that.

Azzie turned to go, but he stopped when an icy finger tapped him on the back. He looked around; the watchman was gone.

An ominous voice said, "Azzie Elbub?"

"Yes. Who's there?"

"Call me Nameless. It seems you've gone and done it again."

"Done what?"

"Produced another unacceptable anomaly."

"Well . . . What's that to you?"

"I'm the Anomaly Eater," Nameless said. "I'm the Special Circumstance that arises in the maw of the universe when things get too hairy. I'm the one Ananke was trying to warn you about. Through your actions you have called me into being."

"I'm sorry to hear that," Azzie said. "I didn't mean to awaken you from your sleep of uncreation. What about if I promise never to produce another anomaly?"

"Not good enough," Nameless said. "You're in for it this time, my lad. You've fooled around with the universal machinery once too often. And while I'm at it, I think I might as well destroy the cosmos and overthrow Ananke and begin everything all over again with me as Supreme Deity."

"That's an overreaction if I ever heard one," Azzie said. "To destroy an anomaly you propose to produce a greater one."

"Well, that's how the universe crumbles," Nameless said. "I'm afraid I'll have to destroy you."

"I suppose you have to try," Azzie said, "but why don't you have it out with Ananke instead? She's top gun around here."

"That's not the way I do business," Nameless said. "I'll start with you. After I've eaten your soul and washed it down with your body, I'll think about who to take on next. That's my agenda."

Chapter 2

Nameless waved what might have been an arm. Before he even had a chance to say good-bye to the watchman, Azzie found himself transported to an outdoor café table in a city whose architecture made it look very much like Rome.

Azzie was impressed by the transition, which Nameless had effected without any visible apparatus, but he was careful not to show his admiration. Nameless seemed to have a swelled head anyway. Nameless was there with him, wearing an overweight human body with a green Tyrolean hat on top of it. A white-coated waiter came over; Azzie ordered a Cinzano and turned to Nameless.

"Okay, now, about this fight. Are we going to have any rules, or is this going to be freestyle all the way?"

Azzie knew he didn't stand a chance against Nameless, whom he suspected of being a just-born superdeity. But he was putting a bold face on it, trying to bluff his way to some advantage.

"Which fighting style are you better at?" Nameless asked.

"I'm known as a master of the contest without rules," Azzie said.

"Is that so? Then I guess we'll have some rules."

Rules were something Azzie knew he could deal with. He had been taking exception to them since he was born, so already he had an advantage. But he was careful not to gloat visibly.

"What rules do you want to fight by?" Nameless said.

Azzie looked around. "Are we in Rome?"

"Yes, we are."

"Then let's go by regulation gladiatorial drill."

No sooner were the words out of his mouth than he had a moment of vertigo. When his head cleared, he found himself standing inside a great amphitheater. Empty seats rose in a circle on all sides of him. Azzie was naked save for a loincloth; apparently the new deity was a bit of a prude. That was worth remembering.

Checking himself over, he saw that he was holding a shield of rather antique design and carrying a standard Roman short sword.

"That was fast," Azzie said.

"I catch on quick," Nameless said, his voice coming from nowhere in particular.

"What now?" Azzie asked.

"Hand-to-hand combat," Nameless said. "Just you and me. Here I come!"

A door slid open on one side of the amphitheater. There was a noisy snarling sound, and out rolled a large metallic object with tracks. Azzie had seen one of these before, during his visits to the First World War battlefields in France. It was a standard-sized army tank with the usual armor and cannon.

"Are you in that tank?" Azzie asked.

"I am the tank," Nameless said.

"Not quite evenly matched, are we?" Azzie said.

"Don't be a sore loser," Nameless said.

The tank rumbled forward, its blue exhaust bleating out a chorus of challenge. Tentacles sprouted from its sides, each tentacle terminating in a whirring buzz saw. Azzie retreated until he felt the wall at his back.

"Wait!" he cried. "Where's the audience?"

"What?" the tank asked, coming to a stop.

"Can't have a real gladiatorial contest without an audience," Azzie said.

The stadium doors opened, and people started to enter the amphitheater. Azzie knew all of them. First came the Greek gods in their sculptured white sheets. Then came Ylith, and with her was Babriel. A few steps behind them came Michael.

Nameless looked them over and apparently didn't like what he saw.

"Just a minute," he said. "A short time-out, okay?"

Azzie found himself in a nineteenth-century sitting room with Nameless.

Chapter 3

"Now, look," Nameless said. "You can see that I've got you outclassed and outmatched. Nothing to be ashamed of. I'm the new paradigm. No one can oppose me. I'm the visible sign of what is to come."

"So kill me and get it over with," Azzie said.

"No, I have a much better idea. I want to let you live. I want you to join me in the new universe I am going to create."

"What do you need me for?"

"I don't. Let's be very clear about that. It's just that once I'm established I'd like to have someone around to talk to. Someone from the good old days, which are now. Someone I didn't create. I suspect it gets boring when there's nobody to talk to but emanations of your own being. I imagine that's why your God went away—He got tired of having nobody to talk to. Nobody from the old days, I mean. Nobody who wasn't Himself in some way or other. I'm not going to make that mistake. You're another point of view, and I can make use of that, so I'd like you to stay on with me."

Azzie was hesitant. It was a great opportunity, of course. But still . . .

"What are you delaying for? I can defeat you utterly, and rather easily, but now I'm giving you a chance to come to my side. You and you alone from this universe, Azzie, will live on after the destruction of everything else. We'll sweep them all away—gods, devils, humans, nature, fate, chance, the whole works. We'll start all over with a jollier cast of characters. You can help me plan it out. We can have it any way we want. You'll be in at the creation of a new universe! You'll be one of its founding fathers. Can't say fairer than that, can I?"

"But everybody else . . ."

"I'm going to kill them all. They all have to go. Don't try to change my mind."

"There's a young boy named Quentin . . ."

"He'll live in your memory."

"There's a witch named Ylith . . ."

"Don't you have a lock of her hair for a keepsake?"

"Can't you keep her alive?" Azzie asked. "And the boy, too? Take the rest."

"Of course I can keep her alive. I can do whatever I want. But I'm not going to let her live. Or the kid. Or anyone else. Only you, Azzie. It's a kind of punishment, you see."

Azzie looked at Nameless. He had the feeling that things weren't going to be much different under the new cosmic management. But he wasn't going to be around to see it. It was time to fight, time to die.

"No, thanks," he said.

Chapter
4

The tank rumbled forward. Now it was a beautiful machine made of an amalgam of anodized aluminum and glowing chrome. White-hot it glowed, and it moved toward Azzie. He dodged out of its way. Due to its melting state, its wheels sagged out of shape and it suddenly had a hard time moving. Nameless hadn't gotten that bit quite right.

The tank fired its cannon. From the cannon's maw came a blobby plastic ball that split upon contact with the sand. Out of it came chiggers and baby mice. All together, they began to dig what looked like a barbecue pit. Azzie was careful not to judge: he didn't know what Nameless had in mind, if anything.

The cannon fired again, but what came out this time was a bunch of notes of the sort musicians write on ruled paper. Azzie could hear Nameless saying, "Cannon, not canon!"

Nameless was having trouble reining in his exuberant imagination. The cannon fired again, and this time it emitted a cascade of multicolored spatter cones, which burbled and gurgled and gave off a noxious fizz.

The tank came into the center of the arena. There was a certain hesitancy about its movements, for it had learned that while Azzie might be negligible as an antagonist, Nameless himself was his own worst enemy. Azzie picked up a stone and prepared to throw it.

And then marching out of Nameless' corner came a host of headless people famous in history: Blackbeard, Anne Boleyn, Lady Jane Grey, the Headless Horseman, John the Baptist, Louis XVI, Marie Antoinette, Mary Stuart, Medusa, Sir Thomas More, and Maximilien de Robespierre. They gathered in a phalanx, their heads tucked under their left arms in a military manner, right arms holding long lances with silvery tips. Robespierre led them, and he said afterward it was the hardest thing he'd ever done in his life.

Azzie called up his own people, who came armed with gross weapons, but they soon faded away. One of Nameless' few rules was that Azzie was going to have to do this alone.

Then Nameless opened a mouth of dirt and boulders and, towering above Azzie, proceeded to snap and bite at him.

"You're crazy!" Azzie cried.

"No," Nameless said. "Why don't you die?"

"You're a poor creation," Azzie said.

"Are you sure we need this combat? Couldn't you just die and have done with it?"

"Sorry," Azzie muttered.

Chapter 5

Azzie looked around. The twelve Olympians, led by Zeus, were sitting on marble steps near to Babriel, Michael, and Ylith. There were new people there, too: Prince Charming and Princess Scarlet, Johann Faust and Marguerite. They rose as one and advanced into the arena.

"This isn't fair!" Nameless said. "You're not allowed to summon help."

"I didn't summon them," Azzie said. "They came on their own."

"I haven't had any time yet to create friends and allies!"

"I know," Ylith said. "You chose to go it alone."

"Too late now," Michael the Archangel said. He stood at the front of the Heavenly hosts. "I think we are all agreed that you, Nameless, are quite unsuited to be Supreme Deity. We're going to join together now and dispose of you."

Then there was a sound of singing, a single strong male voice leading a rousing melody. It was Aretino, singing a Renaissance version of "Onward Christian Soldiers." The chorus was made up of all the others—Quentin and Puss, Kornglow and Leonore, Sir Oliver and Mother Joanna, Rodrigo and Cressilda. They formed a tight circle around the combatants and urged Azzie on. But how silly it was to urge him, he reflected, for there was nothing he could do. The power of this creature from darkest probability had already proven too much for him.

"You don't have to die," Ylith was saying to him. "Ananke is defeated only if you are. You've had the courage to mount your play. Keep fighting!"

Chapter
6

"All right, a little Greco-Roman wrestling," Nameless said, assuming a vaguely human form. "To the death." He seized Azzie in a powerful grip.

Then Quentin cried, "You can't kill him!"

"I can't? Why not?"

"Because he's my friend."

"Young man, you don't seem to realize what an exposed position you're in. I'm the Eater of Souls, my boy. Yours will be like a little maraschino cherry on top of the whipped-cream sundae of this foolish demon here."

"No!" And Quentin smacked Nameless over the head with his open palm. Nameless reared back on his wheels, baring his teeth, and Puss poked the superdeity in the stomach. Nameless collapsed onto the bloody sand. Sir Oliver came into the ring tugging a lance, and with Mother Joanna's help he poked Nameless in the eye.

"Oh, this is too much," Nameless said as the lance passed through his head and he died.

Ananke appeared in the heavens above them, her old lady's face smiling.

"Well done, my children!" she cried. "I knew you could all cooperate, if the cause were dire enough."

"So that's why you hatched this scheme!" Azzie cried.

"One of many reasons, my pet," Ananke said. "There

are always reasons within reasons, and every reason for a reason may itself be scrutinized and its constituent reasons adduced. Don't question it, my friend. You are alive, all of you."

And then they all came together into a dance. They held hands, they mounted to the air. Faster and higher they flew, all of them together, all of them there except . . .

Chapter 7

Aretino suddenly woke with a snort. He sat up in bed and looked out the window. The sun was shining on Venice. Beside him on the bed was a manuscript, *The Legend of the Golden Candlesticks.*

He remembered now that he had dreamed a fantastic dream. That was one explanation.

Another explanation was that Azzie had succeeded in preserving Venice in Limbo.

He looked out the window. People were walking past, Kornglow and Leonore among them.

"What's happening?" Aretino called out.

Kornglow looked up. "Take care, Aretino! They say the Mongols are coming any moment."

So Venice was doomed? Then Aretino knew that everything was all right. What he needed now was to find a quiet place to sit down and continue work on his play.

Aretino woke up on a splendid morning to realize that during the night he had had an unaccountable dream, in which a demon had come to him and ordered him to write a play. The play was about pilgrims and golden candlesticks, and the result so outraged the powers of the universe that Venice was put to destruction. But then Ananke decided to spare it, so the time track of the city that had continued his actions with the demon was cut away and sent to Limbo. And he had awakened in Venice in the real world.

Aretino got up and looked about. Everything looked as it always had. He wondered what was happening to that other Venice, the one in Limbo.

Chapter
8

Fatus felt a certain alarm when he was told that a new place had arrived in Limbo. Limbo was a place of many regions that had been and many that never were. The garden of the Hesperides was here, and Arthur's court of Camelot, and the lost city of Lys.

The new place was Venice, the Venice of Catastrophes, and he went for a walk in this place and marveled at its beauty. The people didn't know it was all fading out, dying, to be renewed again each day. He walked and walked, through scenes of death and dying, and he felt it all very lively. Each day it would start anew. He wished he could tell people that, that there was no reason ever to fear, because in the morning it would all start again. But the people wouldn't listen to him and so lived forever in a state of alarm, starting each day afresh.

Fatus came to the lovers, Kornglow and Leonore. It was refreshing to find two for whom life and the love of each other was a continual revelation and a constant delight. Go and teach the others, he told them, but they only laughed at him. It is simple, how to live, they said. Each can do it, there is nothing to teach.

Fatus returned to his castle and mused over his old things and wondered what might happen next.

Chapter 9

In Venice, the one in Limbo, Kornglow and Leonore talked about Aretino.

"I wonder if he'll ever write his play."

"Perhaps he will. But not the real one. This one—the one in which we die every night, and are reborn every morning. I hope you're not afraid of death, my love."

"Perhaps a little. But we'll be alive again tomorrow, will we not?"

"That is my belief. But death now will feel like death while it is happening."

"Must we die now?"

"All of Venice dies tonight."

There is a clatter of hooves. Horsemen in the city. Mongols!

Kornglow fights valiantly, but he is run through with a lance. The Mongols try to seize Leonore, but she is too quick for them—the Mongol isn't born who can move faster than an elf's daughter. She runs out into the street and plunges into the water, swimming away from the city. The waves are high, walls are falling, and Venice is on fire. She watches for a moment, but she can stay afloat no longer. This is dying for the first time, and though it is difficult, she knows just how to do it. Her head slides beneath the waves.

Chapter
10

Azzie felt a giant hand tightening over him. Then there was blackness. When he awoke, a cool hand was on his brow. He opened his eyes.

"Ylith! What are you doing here? I didn't know demons and witches had any life after death."

"As it happens, you and I are still alive."

Azzie looked around. He was at the Friendly Inn in Limbo, a place of neutrality for spirits Bad and Good.

"What happened to the universe?"

"Thanks to you, Ananke was able to save it. We should all be grateful to you, though I'm afraid you're going to find a lot of people angry. The Council of Evil is considering issuing you a reprimand for starting the whole thing in the first place. But I still care for you. Always will, I'm afraid."

He took her hand.

"Daughter of Darkness," he said, smiling weakly. "We are of a kind."

Nodding, she smiled and squeezed his hand.

"I know," she said.

About the Authors

ROGER ZELAZNY is the author of the Hugo-winning *Lord of Light* and the bestselling *Amber* series, including the classic *Nine Princes of Amber*. He is a six-time Hugo winner and has won three Nebula Awards.

ROBERT SHECKLEY is a novelist and scriptwriter whose short fiction has appeared in *Playboy, The Atlantic Monthly,* and *The Magazine of Fantasy and Science Fiction*. One of his short stories was adapted to film as *The Tenth Victim*.